"If This Is Unsuccessful, Are You Still Willing To Try Again?"

"Of course! I'm in this for the long haul." She yawned deeply, her eyes overflowing with tears. "Well, goodness, all of a sudden I feel exhausted."

She must have slept as poorly as he had last night. Plus she'd had that long drive this morning. "Why don't you close your eyes and rest."

"Maybe just for a minute," she said, her eyes slipping closed. Within minutes her breathing became slow and deep and her lips parted slightly. He sat there looking at her and had the strangest urge to touch her face. To run his finger across her full bottom lip....

He shook away the thought. He hoped this was a one-shot deal. He hoped the test came up positive, not only because he wanted a child, but because he wanted to get the emotionally taxing part of the process out of the way. This entire experience was doing strange things to his head.

Dear Reader,

Welcome to book one of my Black Gold Billionaires series!

I've probably said this before, and at the risk of repeating myself, I just love writing billionaire heroes. But not for the reason you may think. Yes, they're sexy and charming and, yes, they have unlimited resources, but it's more than that. I love that when you peel back the layers, and break down the defenses, they're really just regular guys. They want what everyone wants. Love, acceptance…even if they're too tough or too stubborn to admit it!

That's never been truer than with Adam Blair. He's got it all figured out. He thinks having a child will complete him, fill the hole in his life that has been there since he lost first his mother, then his wife to cancer. What he never counted on was his ex-sister-in-law, Katy Huntly, coming into his life. Not only do opposites attract, they practically combust! But how could two people with practically nothing in common, who want totally different things from life, expect to make a relationship work?

I guess you'll just have to read the book to find out.…

Best,

Michelle

The Tycoon's Paternity Agenda

MICHELLE CELMER

First published in Great Britain 2011
by Mills & Boon, an imprint of Harlequin (UK) Limited.
Large Print edition 2011
Harlequin (UK) Limited,
Eton House, 18-24 Paradise Road,
Richmond, Surrey TW9 1SR

© Michelle Celmer 2010

ISBN: 978 0 263 21784 1

Harlequin (UK) policy is to use papers that are natural, renewable and recyclable products and made from wood grown in sustainable forests. The logging and manufacturing process conform to the legal environmental regulations of the country of origin.

Printed and bound in Great Britain
by CPI Antony Rowe, Chippenham, Wiltshire

MICHELLE CELMER

Bestselling author Michelle Celmer lives in southeastern Michigan with her husband, their three children, two dogs and two cats. When she's not writing or busy being a mom, you can find her in the garden or curled up with a romance novel. And if you twist her arm really hard you can usually persuade her into a day of power shopping.

Michelle loves to hear from readers. Visit her website, www.michellecelmer.com, or write her at P.O. Box 300, Clawson, MI 48017.

To my dad

One

There was no doubt about it, the man was insufferable.

Yet here she was sitting in her pickup truck in the visitors' lot of the Western Oil headquarters building in El Paso, the ruthless, Texas-afternoon sun scorching her face through the windshield.

Katherine Huntley hadn't seen her brother-in-law, Adam Blair, CEO of Western Oil, since her sister's funeral three years ago. His call asking to meet her had come as something of a surprise. It was no shock, however, that he'd had the gall to say he was too busy to meet on her own turf in Peckins, two hours north, and asked her to come to him. But he was the billionaire oil tycoon and she was a lowly cattle rancher, and she was guessing that he was used to people doing things his way.

But that's not why she agreed to come. She was long past overdue for a trip to the warehouse store for supplies anyway, and it gave her the chance to visit the cemetery. Something she did far too infrequently these days. But seeing Rebecca's grave this morning, being reminded once again that Katy had gone from baby sister to only child, brought back the familiar grief. It simply wasn't fair that Becca, who'd had so much to live for, had been taken so young. That her parents had to know the excruciating pain of losing a child.

Katy glanced at the clock on the dash and realized she was about to be late, and since she prided herself on always being punctual, she shoved open her door and stepped out into the blistering heat. It was so hot the soles of her boots stuck to the blacktop. She swiftly crossed the lot to the front entrance, and the rush of icy air as she pushed through the double glass doors into the lobby actually made her shiver.

Considering the suspicious looks the security

guards gave her as she walked through the metal detector, they must not have gotten many women dressed in jeans and work shirts visiting. And, of course, because she was wearing her steel-toe boots, the alarm began to wail.

"Empty your pockets, please," one of them told her.

She was about to explain that her pockets were already empty, when a deep voice ordered, "Let her through."

She looked up to find her brother-in-law waiting just past the security stand, and her heart took a quick dive downward.

Ex-brother-in-law.

Without question the security guards ushered her past, and Adam stepped forward to greet her.

"It's good to see you again, Katy."

"You, too." She wondered if she should hug him, but figured this situation was awkward enough without the burden of unnecessary physical contact, and settled for a handshake instead. But as his hand folded around her own, she wondered if he noticed the calluses and rough skin, not to mention the short, unpainted fingernails. She was sure he was used to women like Rebecca, who spent hours in the salon getting pedicures and manicures, and all the other beauty treatments she neither had time nor the inclination for.

Not that it made a difference what he thought of her nails. But when he released her hand, she stuck them both in her jeans pockets.

In contrast, Adam looked every bit the billionaire CEO that he was. She had nearly forgotten how big he was. Not only did he look as though he spent a lot of time in the weight room, he was above average in height. At five feet nine inches, few men towered over her, but Adam was at least six-four.

He wore his dark hair in the same closely cropped style, although she could see strands of gray peppering his temples now. Of course, as was the case with men like him, it only made him look more distinguished. There were also worry lines at the corners of his eyes and across his forehead that hadn't been there before. Probably from the stress of dealing with Rebecca's illness.

Despite that, he looked good for a man of forty.

Katy was only seventeen when her sister married Adam ten years ago, and though she had never admitted it to a soul, she'd had a mild adolescent crush on her gorgeous new brother-in-law. But neither she nor her parents would have guessed that the charming, handsome man intended to steal Rebecca away from them.

"How was your trip down?" he asked.

She shrugged. "The same as it always is."

She waited for him to explain what she was doing there, or at the very least thank her for making the long drive to see him. Instead he gestured to the shop across the lobby. "Can I buy you a cup of coffee?"

"Sure. Why not?"

Other than the shop employees, everyone seated inside wore business attire, and most had their nose buried in a laptop computer, or a cell phone stuck to their ear. But when Adam entered, everyone stopped what they were doing to nod, or greet him.

Good Lord. When the man entered a room, he owned it. But he was the boss, and it was obvious people respected him. Or feared him.

She followed him to the counter and he spouted some long, complicated-sounding drink to the clerk, then turned to Katy and asked, "What would you like?"

"Plain old black coffee," she told the clerk. She didn't care for the frou-frou blends and flavors that had become so popular lately. Her tastes were as simple as her lifestyle.

With drinks in hand, he led her to a table at the back of the shop. She had just assumed they would go up to his office, but this was okay, too. A little less formal and intimidating. Not that she had a reason to feel intimidated. She didn't know why she was here, so she wasn't really sure what she should be feeling at this point.

When they were seated, Adam asked, "How are your parents? And how are things at the ranch? I trust business is good."

"We're good. I don't know if you heard, but we went totally organic about two years ago."

"That's great. It's the way of the future."

She sipped her coffee. It was hot and strong, just the way she liked it. "But I'm sure you didn't ask me here to talk about cattle."

"No," he agreed. "There's something I need to discuss with you. Something…personal."

She couldn't imagine what personal matter he might have to discuss with her as anything they might have had in common had been buried along with her sister. But she shrugged and said, "Okay."

"I'm not sure if Becca mentioned it, but before she was diagnosed, we had been having fertility issues. Our doctor suggested in vitro, and Becca was going through the hormone therapy to have her eggs extracted when they discovered the cancer."

"She told me." And Katy knew that her sister had felt like a failure for being unable to conceive. She had been terrified of disappointing Adam. Her entire life seemed to revolve around pleasing him. In fact, Becca spent so much time and energy being the perfect high-society wife that she'd had little time left for her family. Adam's schedule had been so busy, they hadn't even come for Christmas the year before she got sick.

If it had been Katy, she would have put her foot down and insisted she see her family. Even if it meant spending the holidays apart from her spouse. Of course, she never would have married a man like Adam in the first place. She could never be with anyone so demanding and self-centered. And especially someone who didn't share her love for the ranch. But according to her parents, practically from the instant Becca left the womb, she had been gunning to move to the city, to live a more sophisticated lifestyle.

Sometimes Katy swore Becca was a doorstep baby.

"She was so sure she would beat it," Adam continued. "We went ahead with our plans, thinking we could hire a surrogate to carry the baby. But, of course, we never got the chance."

"She told me that, too," Katy said, pushing down the bitterness that wanted to bubble to the surface. Harvesting the eggs had meant holding off on treating the cancer, which just might have been the thing that killed her. Katy had begged Becca to forget the eggs and go forward with the treatment. They could always adopt later on, but Becca knew how much Adam wanted a child—his own flesh and blood—and as always, she would have done anything to make him happy.

It would have been easy to blame Adam for her death, but ultimately, it had been Becca's choice. One she had paid dearly for.

"I'm not sure what any of this has to do with me," Katy said.

"I thought you should know that I've decided to use the frozen embryos and hire a surrogate to carry the baby."

He said it so bluntly, so matter-of-factly, it took several seconds for the meaning of his words to sink in.

Baby? Was he saying that he was going to hire some stranger to have her *sister's* child?

Katy was beyond stunned…and utterly speechless. Of all the possible reasons for Adam asking her here, that particular one had never crossed her mind. How could he even consider doing this to her family?

She realized her jaw had fallen and closed her mouth so forcefully her teeth snapped together. Adam was watching her, waiting for her to say something.

Finally she managed, "I…I'm not sure what to say."

"So we're clear, I'm not asking for your permission. Or your approval. Out of courtesy—since it's Rebecca's child, too—I felt I should tell you what I plan to do."

He wasn't the kind of man to do things as a "courtesy." He did nothing unless it benefited him. She was guessing that he'd consulted a lawyer, and his lawyer had advised him to contact Becca's family.

"I also thought you could give me some advice on the best way to break the news to your parents," Adam added, and Katy was too dumbfounded to speak. As if losing their daughter wasn't heartbreaking enough, now they would have to live with the knowledge that they had a grandchild out there with a father who was too busy to even give them the time of day? How could he even think about doing this to them? And then to ask her *help?* Was he really so arrogant? So self-absorbed?

"My advice to you would be don't do it," she told him.

He looked confused. "Don't tell them?"

"Don't use the embryos." She was so angry, her voice was actually shaking. "Haven't my parents been through enough? I can't believe you could be selfish enough to even consider putting them through this."

"I would be giving them a grandchild. A part of their daughter would live on. I'd think that would please them."

"A grandchild they would never see? You really think that's going to make them *happy?*"

"Why would you assume they wouldn't see the baby?"

Was he kidding? "I can count on one hand how many times you and Becca came to visit the last three years of your marriage. My parents were always making the effort, and in most instances you were too busy to make the time for them." She became aware, by the curious stares they were getting, that the volume of her voice had risen to a near-hysterical level. She took a deep breath, forced herself to lower it. "Why not get remarried and have a baby with your new wife? You're a rich, handsome guy. I'm sure women would line up to marry you. Or you could adopt. Just leave my family out of this."

Adam's voice remained calm and even. "As I said, I'm not asking your permission. This meeting was simply a courtesy."

"Bull," she hissed under her breath.

Adam's brow rose. "Excuse me?"

"I'm not some simple, stupid country girl, Adam. So please, don't insult my intelligence by treating me like an uneducated hick. I'm here because your lawyer probably warned you that my parents could fight this, and you want to avoid any legal entanglements."

His expression darkened, and she knew she'd hit a nerve. "Your family has no legal rights over the embryos."

"Maybe not, but if we decided to fight you, it could drag on for years, couldn't it?"

His brow dipped low over his eyes, and he leaned forward slightly. "You don't have the financial means to take me on in court."

Not one to be intimidated, she met his challenge and leaned toward him. "I don't doubt there's some bleeding-heart attorney out there who would just love to take on a case like this pro bono."

He didn't even flinch. Did he know she was bluffing? Not only did she know of no attorney like that, she didn't think her parents would ever try to fight Adam. They would be miserably unhappy, but like Becca's defection from the family fold, they would accept it. And learn to live with it. They didn't like to make waves, to cause problems, which is why they allowed Becca to drift so far from the family in the first place. Had it been up to Katy, things would have been different.

Adam's expression softened and he said in a calm and rational voice, "I think we're getting ahead of ourselves."

"What do you even know about being a parent?" she snapped. "When would you find the time? Have you even considered what you're getting yourself into? Diaper changes and midnight feedings. Or will you hire someone to raise the baby for you? Leave all the dirty work to them?"

"You don't know anything about me," he said.

"Sad, considering you were married to my sister for seven years."

He took a deep breath and blew it out. "I think we got off on the wrong foot here."

Actually, what she had done was reverse the balance of power so that now she had the upper hand. It was the only way to deal with men like him. A trick Becca had obviously never learned.

"Trust me when I say, I have given this considerable thought, and I feel it's something I *need* to do. And I assure you that both you and your parents will see the baby. My parents are both dead, so you'll be the only other family the child has. I would never deny him that."

"And I'm just supposed to believe you?"

"At this point, you really don't have much choice. Because we both know that the chances of finding a lawyer who will represent you for free are slim to none. I've been in business a long time. I recognize a bluff when I see it."

She bit her lip. So much for having the upper hand.

"I'm not doing this to hurt anyone, Katy. I just want a child."

But why did it have to be *Becca's* child? "We may not be as rich as you, but we can still fight it."

"And you would lose."

Yes, she would. But she could put up one hell of a fight. And put her parents through hell in the process. Not to mention decimate them all financially.

The sad fact was she had no choice but to accept this. She was going to have to take him on his word that they would see the baby. What other recourse did she have?

"Can I ask who the surrogate will be?"

He was gracious enough not to gloat at her obvious surrender. "I'm not sure yet. My attorney is looking at possible candidates."

She frowned. "How will you know they're trustworthy?"

"They'll go through a rigorous interview process and background check. If they've ever been arrested, or used illegal substances, we'll know about it."

But there was no way to know everything. Katy watched the national news and knew situations like this had a way of going horribly awry. What if the woman smoked, or did drugs while she was pregnant? Or took some other physical risk that might harm the baby? Or what if she decided she didn't want to give the baby up? Would it matter that it was Rebecca's egg?

Or even worse, she could just disappear with Rebecca's child, never to be seen again. For Katy's parents—and probably Adam, too—it would be like losing Rebecca all over again.

"What if you think the woman is trustworthy, but you're wrong?" she asked him, growing more uneasy by the second.

"We won't be," Adam assured her, but that wasn't good enough.

She took a swallow of her coffee, burning her tongue. If she let him do this, she could look forward to nine months of being on edge, worrying about her niece or nephew's safety.

There was only one person she trusted enough to carry her sister's baby. It was completely crazy, but she knew it was the only way. The only *good* way. And she would do whatever necessary to convince him.

"I know the perfect person to be the surrogate," she told Adam.

"Who?"

"Me."

Two

Adam had imagined several possible scenarios of what Katy's reaction would be when he told her his plans. He thought she might be excited. Grateful even that a part of Rebecca would live on in the baby. He had also considered her being upset, or even indignant, which proved to be much closer to the truth.

But not a single one of those scenarios included her offering to carry the baby herself. And as far as he was concerned, that wasn't an option.

Admittedly he had approached Katy first because he figured she would be easily manipulated, but sweet little Katy had an edge now. She was a lot tougher than she used to be. And she was right about his lawyer's advice. If there were a legal battle over the issue of the embryos, he would win. But it could drag on for years. He didn't want to wait that long. He was ready now. And though allowing her to be the surrogate would significantly ease any opposition from her family, he could see an entire new series of problems arise as a result.

"I can't ask you to do that," he told her.

"You didn't ask. I offered."

"I'm not sure if you fully understand the sacrifice it will be. Physically and emotionally."

"I have friends who have gone through pregnancies, so I know exactly what to expect."

"I imagine that knowing a pregnant person and being one are two very different things."

"I *want* to do it, Adam."

He could see that, but the idea had trouble written all over it. In every language.

He tried a different angle. "How will your… 'significant other' feel about this?"

"That won't be an issue. I see Willy Jenkins occasionally, but he isn't what I would call significant. We're more like…friends with benefits, if you know what I mean."

He did, and for some ridiculous reason he wanted to string this Jenkins guy up by his toes. To him she would always be Rebecca's baby sister. Little Katy.

But Katy was a grown woman. Twenty-seven or -eight, if memory served. It was none of his business who she was friends with.

Or why.

"The process could take a year," he told her. "Longer if it takes more than one try. What if you meet someone?"

"Who the heck am I going to meet? Peckins has a population of eight hundred. Most of the men in town I've known since kindergarten. If I was going to fall madly in love with one of them, I'd have done it by now."

He tried a different angle. "Have you thought of the physical toll it could take on your body?"

"Look who you're talking to," she said, gesturing to her casual clothing, the ash-blond hair pulled back in a ponytail. "I'm not like Rebecca. I don't obsess about my weight, or worry about things like stretch marks. And you won't find anyone more responsible. I don't smoke or take drugs, not even over-the-counter pain relievers. I have an occasional beer, but beyond that I don't drink, so giving it up isn't a problem. Not to mention that I'm healthy as horse. And my doctor never fails to point out at my annual physical that I have a body built for childbearing."

She certainly did. She had the figure of a fifties pinup model. A time when women looked like women, not prepubescent boys. In his opinion Rebecca had always been too obsessed with her weight and her looks, as though she thought he would love her less if she didn't look perfect 100 percent of the time. Even during chemo she never failed to drag herself out of bed to put on makeup. And when she could no longer get out of bed, she had the nurse do it for her.

The familiar stab of pain he felt when he thought of her that way pierced the shell around his heart from the inside out.

Katy surprised him by reaching across the table and taking his hand. What surprised him even more was the tingling sensation that started in his fingers and worked its way up his arm. Her hands were a little rough from working on the ranch, but her skin was warm. Her nails were bare, but clean and neatly trimmed. Everything about her was very…natural.

Which was more than he could say for this situation, and the odd, longing sensation deep in his gut.

"Adam, you know as well as I do that despite all the background checks you can do, there's no one you could trust as much as me."

He hated to admit it—she was right. Despite their very complicated past and feelings of resentment over Becca, Katy would never do anything to put her sister's child in harm's way. But she could use the opportunity to try to manipulate him, and he never put himself in a position to lose the upper hand. Not professionally, and especially not personally.

Not anymore.

But this was the welfare of his child they were discussing. Wasn't it his obligation as a father to put his child first, to make its health and well-being his number-one priority?

Katy squeezed his hand so tight he started to lose sensation in his fingers, and they were beginning to get curious glances from his employees.

He gently extracted his hand from hers. "Look, Katy—"

"Please, Adam. Please let me do this." She paused, her eyes pleading, then said, "You know it's what Becca would have wanted."

Ouch. That was a low blow, and she knew how to hit where it really stung. The worst part was that she was right. Didn't he owe it to Becca to let Katy do this for them? For the baby? Wasn't he partially to blame for Becca losing touch with her family in the first place?

"Though it's against my better judgment, and I would like to run it past my attorney before I give you a definitive answer...I'm inclined to say yes."

Her expression was a combination of relief and gratitude. "Thank you, Adam. I promise, you won't regret this."

Impossible, since he regretted it already.

Katy left soon after, and Adam headed back up to his office, feeling conflicted.

On one hand he could see the benefits of choosing Katy as a surrogate. In theory, it was an ideal arrangement. But he knew from experience that things did not always go as planned, and what may seem "ideal" one day could swiftly become a disaster the next.

Before he made any decisions, he would speak with his attorney.

His assistant, Bren, stopped him as he walked past her desk to his office. "Senator Lyons called while you were gone. He said he'll be out of the office the rest of the day but he'll call you back tomorrow."

"Did he say what he wanted?"

"My guess would be a campaign contribution. Isn't he up for reelection?"

"You're probably right."

"Also, Mr. Suarez needs to see you when you have a minute."

"Call down to his office and tell him now would be good," he told her. It was doubtful he would be able to concentrate on work anyway. Too much on his mind.

He stepped into his office, stopped at the wet bar to pour himself a scotch, then sat behind his desk and booted his computer.

"Hey, boss."

He looked up to find Emilio Suarez, Western Oil CFO, standing in his open doorway.

Western Oil was in dire financial straits when Adam inherited it from his father, and Emilio's financial genius had brought it back from the brink of ruin. Though he was from a Puerto Rican family of modest means, through grants and scholarships Emilio had graduated college at the top of his class, which was what had caught Adam's attention when he was looking for a management team. Emilio had become an irreplaceable employee—not to mention a good friend—and worth every penny of his ridiculously exorbitant salary.

Adam gestured him inside. "You wanted to talk to me?"

He came in, shutting the door behind him, and stopped to pour himself a drink. "I got an interesting call from my brother today."

"The federal prosecutor, the one in Europe or the other brother?"

The "other" brother was the family black sheep. A drifter who only called when he needed something. Money usually. For bail, or to pay off loan sharks.

"The prosecutor," he said, taking a seat opposite Adam's desk. "And if anyone asks, you did not hear this from me."

"Of course."

"You know Leonard Betts?"

"By reputation only." He was a financial wizard and according to Forbes, the richest man in Texas. It had been said that everything he touched turned to gold.

"You ever invest with him?" Emilio asked.

He shook his head. "He always seemed a little too successful, if you know what I mean. Either he's extremely lucky—and luck can run out—or he's shady."

"You've got good instincts. According to Alejandro, he's been under investigation by the SEC, and it's looking like he and his wife will be arrested and charged for a Ponzi scheme."

Adam shook his head in disbelief. "His wife, too?"

"And her parents. Or at least, her mother. Her father died a few years ago."

"So it was a family business."

"I guess. I just thought I should warn you that, although it's unlikely, there's the slightest possibility that when the media gets wind of this, my name may come up."

Adam sat straighter in his seat. "You've invested with him?"

"No! No, my market is real estate. This is more of personal connection."

Adam frowned, not sure he was liking what he was hearing. It would be in the company's best interest to stay as far removed as possible from this scandal. "How personal?"

"In college, I was engaged to Isabelle Winthrop. Betts's wife."

Adam's jaw nearly fell. Emilio had never mentioned knowing her, much less being engaged to her. Or anyone for that matter. He was so fiercely against the entire institution of marriage, Adam wouldn't have guessed that he would have been planning a trip to the altar with any woman. "I had no idea."

"She dumped me for Betts two weeks before we planned to elope."

"Damn. I'm really sorry, Emilio."

Emilio shrugged. "Honestly, she did me a favor.

We were young and stupid. We would have been divorced in a year."

Something in his eyes told Adam he was making light of an otherwise painful situation. But he didn't push the issue. If Emilio wanted to talk about it, he knew Adam was there for him.

"There's no doubt she was a gold digger, but I'll be honest, I never imagined her capable of helping Leonard bilk his clients out of millions of dollars."

"Well, if your name does come up, we'll use Cassandra."

Cassandra Benson was Western Oil's public relations director. For her, media spin was an art form. If properly motivated, she could make climate change sound environmentally beneficial.

"So," Emilio said, leaning back in his chair and taking a swallow of his drink. "What's this I hear about you and a mystery woman?"

"Wow, good news travels fast." He should have taken Katy up to his office. It was just that the coffee shop seemed more...neutral. He should have known better and met her somewhere off campus and far from the building. Like California.

"The CEO can't sit in the company coffee shop holding hands with a woman no one has seen before, and expect it to go unnoticed."

"Well, she's not a mystery woman. She's my sister-in-law. And we weren't holding hands. We were talking."

"I thought you didn't see Becca's family any longer."

"I haven't in a long time. But something has come up."

"Is everything okay?"

Up until today, Adam hadn't talked to anyone but his attorney and the fertility doctor about his baby plan, but he knew he could trust Emilio to keep it quiet. So he told him, and his reaction was about what Adam would have expected.

"Wow," Emilio said, shaking his head in disbelief. "I didn't even know you wanted kids. I mean, I knew that you and Rebecca were trying, but I had no idea you would want to be a single father."

"It's something I've wanted for a while. It just feels like the right time to me. And since I don't plan to get married again…" He shrugged. "Surrogacy seems to be my best option."

"Why the meeting with Becca's sister...I'm sorry, I don't recall her name."

"Katherine...Katy. I called her as a courtesy, and on the advice of my attorney."

"So, what did she say?"

"She wants to be the surrogate."

One brow rose. "Seriously?"

"Yeah. In fact, she was pretty adamant about it. She claims that she's the only person I can trust."

"Do you trust her?"

"I believe that she would never do anything to harm Becca's baby."

"But..."

"Katy seems very...headstrong. If I hire someone, I'll be calling the shots. Katy on the other hand is in a position to make things very complicated."

"Correct me if I'm wrong, but if you tell her no, she could make things complicated, too."

"Exactly."

"So you're damned if you do and damned if you don't."

"More or less." And he didn't like being backed into a corner.

"So what did you tell her?"

"That I had to talk to my attorney."

"You hear so many horror stories about surrogacy agreements going bad. Just a few weeks ago Alejandro was telling me about a case in New Mexico. A couple hired a surrogate to carry their baby. She was Hispanic, and halfway through the pregnancy moved back to Mexico and dropped off the map. Unfortunately the law is in her favor."

Adam had heard similar cautionary tales.

"I think, if you have someone you can trust, let her do it," Emilio said.

He would make the call to his attorney, to check on the legalities of it and his rights as the father, but Emilio was right. Choosing Katy just made the most sense. And ultimately the benefits would outweigh the negatives.

He hoped.

Three

What the hell was he doing here?

The limo pitched and swayed up the pitted, muddy gravel road that led to the Huntley's cattle ranch, and Adam lunged to keep the documents he'd been reading on the ride up from sliding off the leather seat and scattering to the floor.

His driver and bodyguard, Reece, would have to take a trip to the car wash as soon as they got back to El Paso, Adam realized as he gazed out the mud-splattered window. At least the torrential rain they'd encountered an hour ago had let up and now there was nothing but blue sky for miles.

As they bounced forward up the drive, Adam

could see that not much had changed in the four years since he'd last been here. The house, a typical, sprawling and rustic ranch, was older, but well maintained. Pastures with grazing cattle stretched as far as the eye could see.

The ranch had been in their family for five generations. A tradition Becca had had no interest in carrying on. As far as she had been concerned, Katy could have it all.

And now she would.

The limo rolled to a stop by the front porch steps and Reece got out to open his door. As he did, a wall of hot, damp air engulfed the cool interior, making the leather feel instantly sticky to the touch.

This meeting had been Katy's idea, and he wasn't looking forward to it. Not that he disliked his former in-laws. He just had nothing in common with them. However, if they were going to be involved in his child's life, the least he could do was make an effort to be cordial. According to Katy, the news of his plan to use the embryos had come as a shock to them, but knowing Katy would be the surrogate had softened the blow. And since a meeting with his attorney last week, when he and Katy signed a surrogacy agreement, it was official. With any luck, nine months from her next ovulation cycle she would be having his and Becca's baby.

After months of consideration and planning, it was difficult to believe that it was finally happening. That after years of longing to have a child, he finally had his chance. And despite Katy and her parents' concerns, he would be a good father. Unlike his own father, who had been barely more than a ghost after Adam's mother passed away. Adam spent most of his childhood away at boarding schools, or in summer camps. The only decent thing his father had ever done was leave him Western Oil when he died. And though it had taken several years of hard work, Adam had pulled it back from the brink of death.

"Sir?"

Adam looked up and realized Reece was standing by the open car door, waiting for him to climb out.

"Everything okay, sir?" he asked.

"Fine." May as well get this over with, he thought, climbing from the back of the car into the sticky heat.

"Hey, stranger," he heard someone call from the vicinity of the barn, and looked over to see Katy walking toward him. She was dressed for work, her thick, leather gloves and boots caked with mud. Her hair was pulled back into a pony-tail and as she got closer he saw that there was a smudge of dirt on her left cheek. For some odd reason he felt the urge to reach up and rub it clean.

He looked her up and down and asked, "Am I early? I was sure you said four o'clock."

"No, you're right on time. The rain set us back in our chores a bit, that's all." She followed his gaze down her sweat-soaked shirt and mud-splat-tered jeans and said apologetically, "I'd hug you, but I'm a little filthy."

Filthy or not, he wasn't the hug type. "I'll settle for a handshake."

She tugged off her glove and wiped her hand on the leg of her jeans before extending it to him. Her skin was hot and clammy, her grip firm. She turned to Reece and introduced herself. "Kath-erine Huntley, but everyone calls me Katy."

He warily accepted her outstretched hand. He wasn't used to being acknowledged, much less greeted so warmly. Adam recalled that the hired help had always been regarded as family on the Huntley ranch. "Reece Wilson, ma'am."

"It's a scorcher. Would you like to come inside with us?" she asked, gesturing to the house. "Have something cold to drink?"

"No, thank you, ma'am."

"If you're worried about your car," she said with a grin, "I promise no one will steal it."

Was she actually flirting with his driver? "He's fine," Adam said. "And we have a lot to discuss."

Her smile dissolved and there was disapproval in her tone when she said, "Well, then, come on in."

He followed her up the steps to the porch, where she kicked off her muddy boots before opening the door and gesturing him inside. A small vestibule opened up into the great room and to the left were the stairs leading to the second floor.

The furniture was still an eclectic mix of styles and eras. Careworn, but comfortable. The only modern addition he could see was the large, flat-screen television over the fireplace. Not much else had changed. Not that he'd been there so often he would notice small differences. He could count on two hands how many times they had visited in the seven years he and Becca were married. Not that he hadn't wanted to, despite what Katy and her parents believed.

"My parents wanted to be here to greet you, but they were held up at a cattle auction in Bellevue," Katy told him. "They should be back within the hour."

He had hoped to get this business out of the way, so he could return to El Paso at a decent hour. Though it was Friday, he had a long work-day ahead of him tomorrow.

"Would you like a cold drink?" she asked. "Iced tea or lemonade?"

"Whatever is easiest."

Katy turned toward the door leading to the kitchen and hollered, "Elvie! You in there?"

Several seconds passed, then the door slid open several inches and a timid looking Hispanic girl who couldn't have been a day over sixteen peered out. When she saw Adam standing there her eyes widened, then lowered shyly, and she said in a thick accent, "*Sí,* Ms. Katy."

"Elvie, this is Mr. Blair. Could you please fetch

him something cold to drink, and take something out to his driver, too?"

She nodded and slipped silently back into the kitchen.

Katy looked down at her filthy clothes. "I'm a mess. I hope you don't mind, but I'm going to hop into a quick shower and get cleaned up."

"By all means." It wasn't as if he was going anywhere. Until her parents returned he was more or less stuck there.

"I'll just be a few minutes. Make yourself at home."

She left him there and headed up the stairs. With nothing to do but wait, Adam walked over to the hearth, where frame after frame of family photos sat. Adam had very few photos of his own family, and only one of his mother.

In his father's grief, he'd taken down all the pictures of Adam's mother after her death and stored them with the other family antiques and keepsakes in the attic of his El Paso estate. A few years later, when Adam was away at school and his father traveling in Europe, faulty wiring started a fire and the entire main house burned to the ground. Taking whatever was left of his mother with it.

At the time it was just one more reason in an ever-growing list to hate his father. When Adam got the call that he'd died, he hadn't talked to the old man in almost five years.

He leaned in to get a closer look at a photo of Becca that had been taken at her high school graduation. She looked so young. So full of promise. He'd met her only a few years later. Her college roommate was the daughter of a family friend and Becca had accompanied them to his home for a cocktail party. Though Adam had been a decade older, he'd found her completely irresistible, and it was obvious the attraction was mutual. Though it had been against his better judgment, he asked her out, and was genuinely surprised when she declined. Few women had ever rejected his advances.

She found him attractive, she said, but needed to focus all her energy on school. She had a plan, she'd told him, a future to build, and she wouldn't stray from that. Which made him respect her even more.

But he wasn't used to taking no for an answer,

either, so he'd persisted, and finally she agreed to one date. But only as friends. He took her to dinner and the theater. She hadn't even kissed him goodnight, but as he drove home, he knew that he would eventually marry her. She was everything he wanted in a wife.

They saw each other several times before she finally let him kiss her, and held out for an excruciating three months before she would sleep with him. He wouldn't say that first time had been a disappointment, exactly. It had just taken a while to get everything working smoothly. Their sex life had never been what he would call smoking hot anyway. It was more...comfortable. Besides, their relationship had been based more on respect than sex. And he preferred it that way.

They were seeing each other almost six months before she admitted her humble background— not that it had made a difference to him—and it wasn't until they became engaged a year later that she finally introduced him to her family.

After months of hearing complaints about her family, and how backward and primitive ranch life was, he'd half expected to meet the modern equivalent of the Beverly Hillbillies, but her parents were both educated, intelligent people. He never really understood why she resented them so. Her family seemed to adore her, yet she always made excuses why they shouldn't visit, and the longer she stayed away, the more her resentment seemed to grow. He had tried to talk to her about it, tried to reason with her, but she would always change the subject.

Elvie appeared in the kitchen doorway holding a glass of lemonade. Eyes wary, she stepped into the room and walked toward the sofa. He took a step in her direction to take the glass from her, and she reacted as if he'd raised a hand to strike her. She set the drink down on the coffee table with a loud clunk then scurried back across the room and through the kitchen door.

"Thank you," he said to her retreating form. He hoped she was a better housekeeper than a conversationalist. He picked up the icy glass and raised it to his lips, but some of the lemonade had splashed over and it dripped onto the lapel of his suit jacket.

Damn it. There was nothing he hated more than stains on his clothes. He looked around for something to blot it up, so it didn't leave a permanent mark. He moved toward the kitchen, to ask Elvie for a cloth or towel, but given her reaction to him, he might scare her half to death if he so much as stepped through the door. He opted for the second floor bathroom instead, which he vaguely recalled to be somewhere along the upstairs hallway.

He headed up the stairs and when he reached the top step a grayish-brown ball of fur appeared from nowhere and wrapped itself around his ankles, nearly tripping him. He caught the banister to keep from tumbling backward.

Timid housekeepers and homicidal cats. What could he possibly encounter next?

He gave the feline a gentle shove with the toe of his Italian-leather shoe, which he noticed was dotted with mud, and shooed it away. It meowed in protest and darted to one of the closed doors, using its weight to shove it open. Wondering if that could be the bathroom he was searching for, he crossed the hall and peered inside. But it wasn't the bathroom. It was Katy's room. She stood beside the bed, wearing nothing but a bath towel, her hair damp and hanging down her back.

Damn.

She didn't seem to notice him there so he opened his mouth to say something, to warn her of his presence, but it was too late. Before he could utter a sound, she tugged the towel loose and dropped it to the wood floor.

And his jaw nearly went with it. He tried to look away, knew he *should* look away, but the message wasn't making it to his brain.

Her breasts were high and plump, the kind made just for cupping, with small, pale pink nipples any man would love to get his lips around. Her hips were the perfect fullness for her height. In fact, she was perfectly proportioned. Becca had been rail thin and petite. Almost nymph-like. Katy was built like a *woman.*

Then his eyes slipped lower and he saw that she clearly was a natural blonde.

It had been a long time since he'd seen a woman naked, so the sudden caveman urge he was feeling to put his hands on her was understandable. But this was Katy. His wife's baby sister.

The thing is, she was no baby.

A droplet of water leaked from her hair and rolled down the generous swell of her breast. He watched, mesmerized as it caught on the crest of her nipple, wondering if it felt even half as erotic as it looked.

Katy cleared her throat, and Adam realized that at some point during his gawking she had realized he was there. He lifted his eyes to hers and saw that she was watching him watch her.

Rather than berate him or try to cover herself—or both, since neither would be unexpected at this point—she just stood there wearing a look that asked what the heck he thought he was doing.

Why the hell wasn't she covering herself? Was she an exhibitionist or something? Or maybe the more appropriate question was, why was he still looking?

She planted her hands on her hips, casual as can be, and asked. "Was there something you needed?"

He had to struggle to keep his eyes on hers, when they naturally wanted to stray back down to her breasts. "I was looking for the bathroom, then there was this cat, and it opened your door."

"Right."

"This was an accident." A very unfortunate, wonderful accident.

"If that's true, then I think at this point the

gentlemanly thing to do would be to turn around. Don't you?"

"Of course. Sorry." He swiftly turned his back to her. What the hell was wrong with him? He never got flustered, but right now he was acting like a sex-starved adolescent. She must have thought he was either a pervert, or a complete moron. "I don't know what I was thinking. I guess I *wasn't* thinking. I was…surprised. I apologize."

"Try two doors down on the right," she said from behind him, closer now. So close he was sure that if he turned, he could reach out and touch her. He pictured himself doing just that. He imagined the weight of her breast in his palm, the taste of her lips as he pressed his mouth to hers.…

He nearly groaned, the sudden ache in his crotch was so intense. What the hell was the matter with him? "Two doors down?"

"The bathroom. You were looking for it, right?"

"Right," he said, barely getting the words out without his voice cracking. He forced his feet forward.

Since Becca's death he'd barely thought about

sex, but now it would seem that his libido had lurched into overdrive.

"And, Adam?" she added.

He paused, but didn't dare turn back around. "Yes?"

"For the record, if you wanted to see me naked, all you had to do was ask."

Four

Oh, good Lord in heaven.

Katy closed her bedroom door and leaned against it, heart throbbing in her chest, legs as weak as a newborn calf's. The sudden and unexpected heat at the apex of her thighs…heaven help her, she might actually self-combust. It was as unexpected as it was mortifying.

The way Adam had looked at her, the fire in his eyes…she couldn't even recall the last time a man had looked at her that way. Hell, she wasn't sure if anyone *ever* had.

She pinched her eyes shut and squeezed her legs together, willing it away, but that only made it worse. An adolescent crush was one thing, but this? It couldn't be more wrong. Or inappropriate. He was her brother-in-law. Her sister's *husband.* The father of the child she would eventually be carrying.

Not to mention that she didn't even *like* him. He was overbearing and arrogant, and generally not a very nice person.

At least she knew that he wasn't lying about seeing her being an accident. Her bedroom door didn't latch correctly and her cat, Sylvester, was always letting himself in. If she had known Adam was going to be wandering around upstairs she would have been more careful. And maybe making that crack about Adam only having to ask wasn't her smartest move, but she refused to let him know how rattled she was.

Not that she was ashamed of the way she looked. As bodies went, hers wasn't half-bad. She just never planned on Adam ever seeing it. Not outside of the delivery room anyway.

She just hoped he never took her up on her offer.

Of course he wouldn't! He was no more inter- ested in her than she was in him. Not only were they ex in-laws, but they were polar opposites. They didn't share a single thing in common as far as she could tell. Except maybe sexual attraction. But that was fleeting, and superficial. Like her on-again off-again relationship with Willy Jenkins used to be. He was a pretty good kisser, and fun under the covers, but he wasn't known for his stimulating conversation. As her best friend Missy would say, he was nice to visit, but she wouldn't want to live there.

Not that Katy would be "visiting" Adam. She would have to be pretty hard up to sleep with a man she had no affection for. She couldn't imagine ever being that desperate.

She heard a vehicle out front and peered through the curtains to see her parents' truck pull up in front of the barn. Well, shoot! Now she had to go out there and act like nothing happened. Which technically it hadn't.

She yanked on clean jeans and a T-shirt and pulled her damp hair back in a ponytail. As she tugged on her cowboy boots she heard the side kitchen door slam, then the muffled sound of voices from the great room below. She had talked Adam into this visit, so it didn't seem fair making him face her parents alone. And at the same time, she was dreading this. She didn't like to play the role of the mediator. That had always been her mother's thing.

In the week since she had talked Adam into letting her be the surrogate, Katy had been working on convincing her parents that she was doing the right thing, and that they were going to have to trust Adam. She just hoped that seeing him face-to-face didn't bring back a flood of the old resentment.

At first, when they learned that Becca was engaged, besides being stunned that she'd never mentioned a steady man in her life, her parents had been truly excited about having a son-in-law. But from the minute they met Adam it was obvious he came from a different world. And as hard as they tried to be accepting, to welcome him to the family, it seemed he always held something back. Her parents interpreted it as Adam thinking he was better than them, even though he had always been gracious enough not to condescend, or treat them with anything but respect.

At first Katy had given him the benefit of the doubt. She wanted to believe that he was as amazing as her sister described. But when he and Becca visited less and less, and Katy realized just how hard Becca had to work to keep him happy, she'd had to face the truth. Adam was an arrogant, controlling and critical husband.

But Katy wasn't doing this for him. She was doing it for Becca, and her parents, and most of all the baby. Which made what just happened between them seem wholly insignificant. It was a fluke, that's all. One that would never happen again.

She headed down the stairs to the great room. Her parents sat stiffly on the sofa and Adam looked just as uncomfortable on the love seat opposite them. When she entered the room everyone turned, looking relieved to see her.

"Sorry to keep you waiting," she told Adam, and his expression gave away no hint of their earlier...confrontation. Although he might have snuck a quick look at her breasts.

"Your parents and I have had a chance to get reacquainted," he said, and from the vibe in the room, Katy could guess it hadn't exactly gone well.

So as not to be antagonistic and give anyone

the impression she was taking sides, she sat by neither her parents nor Adam, but instead on the hearth between them.

The contrast was staggering. Adam looked cool and confident in his suit, like he was ready to negotiate a million-dollar deal, while her parents looked like...well, like they always had. Her father had gotten a little paunchy over the past few years, and his salt-and-pepper hair was thinning at his temples, but he still looked pretty good for a man of sixty-two. And as far as Katy was concerned, her mother, fifty-nine on her next birthday, was as beautiful as she'd been at sixteen. She was still tall, slender and graceful with the face of an angel. She wore her gray-streaked, pale blond hair in loose waves that hung to just above her waist, or at times pulled back in a braid.

She was a perpetually happy person, always preferring to see the glass not only as half full, but the ideal temperature, as well. But now creases of concern bracketed her eyes.

"I was just telling Adam how surprised we were when we heard of his plans," her father said, and his tone clearly said he didn't like it much.

Katy's mom rested a hand on his knee then told Adam, "But we're hoping you can convince us that you've thought this through, and taken our family into consideration."

Katy bit her lip, praying that Adam's first reaction wasn't to get defensive. What had he told Katy that day in the coffee shop? That he wasn't seeking anyone's approval or permission? But he had to expect this, didn't he? He had to know her parents would be wary. That was the whole point of his visit. To set their minds at ease.

Or maybe he didn't see it that way. Maybe he truly didn't give a damn what they thought.

"As I told Katy, I have no intention of keeping the child from you," he assured them, in a tone that showed no hint of impatience, and Katy went limp with relief. "You'll be his or her only grandparents. In fact, I think that spending time on the ranch will be an enriching experience."

"I'm also not sure I like the idea of Katy being your surrogate," her father added, and suddenly everyone looked at her.

"I have my concerns as well, Mr. Huntley. But she wouldn't take no for an answer."

"I think we all know how stubborn she can

be," her father said, talking about her as though she wasn't sitting right there. "I'd like to see her concentrate on finding a husband, and having kids of her own."

She was so sick of that tired old argument. Just because practically every other woman in her family married young and immediately started squeezing out babies, that didn't mean it was right for her.

"I'm not ready for a husband or kids," she told her father. Or more accurately, they weren't ready for her. Every time she thought she'd found Mr. Right, he turned out to be Mr. Right Now, then inevitably became Mr. Last Week. She was beginning to suspect that these men who kept breaking her heart knew something she didn't. Like maybe she just wasn't marriage material.

"You might feel differently when you meet the right man," he countered. "And besides, I don't think you realize how hard this will be. And what if, God forbid, something happens, then you can't have kids of your own? You could regret it the rest of your life."

"What if I walk out the door and get hit by

lightning?" she snapped. "Do you expect me to stop going outside?"

He cast her a stern look, and she bit her tongue.

"Gabe," her mother said gently. "You know that my pregnancies were completely uneventful. And Katy has always been just like me. She'll do fine. You have to admit it will be nice to have a grand-baby." Moisture welled in the corners of her eyes. "To have a part of Rebecca with us."

"I assure you that Katy will have the best pre-natal care available," Adam told them. "We won't let anything happen to her."

The way he hadn't let anything happen to Becca?

The question hung between them unspoken. It was hard not to blame Adam for Becca's death. Though he had done everything within his power to save her. She had seen the best doctors, re-ceived the most effective, groundbreaking treat-ment money could buy. Unfortunately it hadn't been enough.

If she hadn't insisted they harvest the damned eggs...

"What about multiples?" her father asked.

"She's not going to be like that octo-mom and have eight babies."

"Absolutely not. The doctor has already made it clear that for a woman Katy's age, with no prior fertility issues, he won't implant more that two embryos at a time. And if Katy is uncomfortable with the idea of carrying twins, we'll only implant one. It's her call."

"But the odds are better if they implant two?" Katy asked.

"Yes."

"So we'll do two."

"You're sure?" Adam asked. "Maybe you should take some more time to think about it."

"I don't need time. I'm sure."

"Could you imagine that?" her mother said. "Two grandbabies!"

"I still don't like it," her father said, then he looked at his wife and his expression softened. "But it wouldn't be the first time the women in this family have overruled me."

"So it's settled," Katy said, before he could change his mind, with a finality that she hoped stuck this time.

"When will this happen?" Katy's mom asked.

"We have an appointment with a fertility specialist next Wednesday," Adam told her. "First he has to do a full exam and determine if she's healthy enough to become pregnant. Then he'll determine the optimal time for the implantation."

"So if everything looks good, it could be soon," Katy said, feeling excited. "I could be pregnant as soon as next month."

"And if it doesn't work?" her father asked.

"We try again," Adam said. "If we do two embryos at a time, we can do three implantations."

"It sounds so simple," her mother said, but Katy knew things like this were never as simple as they sounded. That didn't mean they weren't worth doing.

"And if none of them take?" Katy asked.

"I'll consider adoption."

"We appreciate you coming all the way out here to talk to us," her mother said. "I know it's eased my mind."

Adam looked at his watch. "But I should be going. I need to get back to El Paso."

"But you just got here," Katy said, surprised that after such a long drive he would want to get back on the road so soon. Was he really so uncomfortable there that he couldn't stick around for a couple of hours? What would he do when the baby was born? Would they always be coming to him?

"The least we can do is feed you supper," her mother said.

"I appreciate the offer, but I have an important meeting Monday that I need to prepare for. Maybe some other time."

They all knew those were just polite words. There wouldn't be another time. He wouldn't be coming back if he could possibly avoid it.

Katy rose to her feet. "I'll walk you out."

He said a somewhat stiff goodbye to her parents, then followed Katy out the front door. The moist heat was almost suffocating as they stepped out onto the porch. Adam's driver had taken refuge in the limo and was reading a newspaper, but when he saw them emerge he swiftly opened his door and got out. Katy turned to Adam, thinking that he had to be roasting in his suit and anxious to get back into the cool car.

"Thanks again for coming all the way out here. And thanks for being so patient with my father." It had to be doubly weird for him, trying to convince her parents she would be a good surrogate, when he himself still had doubts.

"It wasn't quite as bad as I thought it would be. Knowing your father holds me responsible for Becca's death, I realize it can't be easy for him to entrust me with the care of his only living child."

"Why would you think that?" she asked, although for the life of her she didn't know why she gave a damn what he believed.

He gave her a "spare me" look. "Not that I blame him. I should have been able to save her."

"Sounds like maybe it's *you* who holds you responsible."

If her words bothered him, he didn't let on. "I've made my peace with Becca's death."

"Your actions would suggest otherwise, Adam."

He looked at her for a second, like he might say something else, something snarky, then he seemed to change his mind. He turned and walked down the steps. Reece opened the rear car door, but before he got in, Adam turned back to her.

"By the way, I wanted to apologize again, for what happened upstairs."

She folded her arms under her breasts. "You mean when you stared at me while I was naked?"

Reece's eyes widened for an instant, before he caught himself and wiped the surprised look off his face. And if she'd embarrassed Adam—which was the whole point—he didn't let it show. Was he a robot or something? Devoid of human feelings?

"Yes, that," he said.

She shrugged. "It's been stared at before."

"Don't forget we have an appointment with Dr. Meyer on Wednesday at 3:00 p.m."

She snorted. "Like I could forget that."

"I'll see you Wednesday," he said and she could swear he almost smiled. She found herself wishing he would, so he would seem more…human. Maybe he forgot how.

He may have been an overbearing, arrogant, narcissistic jerk, but that didn't mean he deserved to be unhappy. Although he hadn't looked unhappy earlier, when he was standing in her bedroom doorway. He looked like he wanted to throw her down on the bed and have his way with her, which, let's face it, was never going to happen.

He got in the car, and Reece closed the door. Katy waved as they pulled down the driveway. The windows were tinted so she couldn't tell if Adam was watching, but she had the feeling he was. When they turned onto the road and disappeared out of sight, she crossed the porch to the side door around the corner...and almost plowed into her mom, who was pulling on her mucking boots.

Katy squeaked in surprise and skidded to a stop, hoping she hadn't heard that comment about Adam seeing her naked.

"Going out to the barn?" she asked brightly. A little *too* brightly if her mother's wry expression was any indication.

"Be careful, Katy," she said and it was obvious she *had* heard. "When you fall, it's hard and fast."

Fall? *For Adam?* Ugh. Not in a million years. She had clearly taken what was said *completely* out of context. "It's not what you think. He was looking for the bathroom and saw me getting dressed. It was an accident. What I said just now, that was only to embarrass him."

She didn't look convinced. "I know you always had a bit of a crush on him."

"For pity's sake! When I was a *kid.* Not only do I not have a crush, but I don't even *like* him."

"He's not like us, Katy."

Didn't she know it. "You're preaching to the choir, Mom."

"I just want you to consider this carefully. When you're pregnant, and your hormones are all out of whack, those emotional lines can get… fuzzy."

"I'm not going to fall for Adam. It's not even a remote possibility."

She didn't look like she believed Katy, but she let it drop.

The idea of her and Adam in a relationship was beyond ridiculous. Her mother had to know that.

Or was she seeing something that Katy wasn't?

Five

Adam met Katy at the doctor's office Wednesday as planned. She got there first, and as he walked into the lobby he was a bit taken aback when he saw her. In fact, until she smiled and waved, he didn't even realize it *was* her. Dressed in a white-cotton peasant blouse and a caramel-colored ankle-length skirt, she looked like…a woman. She'd even traded in the her usual pony-tail for soft, loose ringlets that framed her face and draped across her shoulders. Even he couldn't deny that the effect was breathtaking.

He had always considered her attractive, but now she looked…well, frankly, she looked *hot*.

It was only the third time in his life that he'd seen her wear anything but jeans and boots. The first was his wedding, and the second Becca's funeral, but neither time had he been paying attention to how she looked. Was it possible that she'd always looked this blatantly sexy and he'd just never noticed?

And today, he wasn't the only one. Heads were turning as she walked past, eyes following her with obvious appreciation. But he knew something they didn't. He knew that as good as she looked in her clothes, she looked even better out of them.

A fact he'd been trying to forget all week.

Katy on the other hand seemed oblivious to the looks she was getting, as though she didn't have even the slightest idea how pretty she was. Or more likely, didn't care either way. He'd never met a woman so casual about her self-image. As evidenced, he realized with a tug of humor, by the fact that under the skirt she was wearing cowboy boots.

He could take the woman out of the country, but not the country out of the woman.

"You're early," he said as she approached him.

"I know, I didn't want to risk being late," she told him, then added, as if she thought he wouldn't notice on his own, "I wore my girl clothes."

"So you did."

"I'm *really* nervous."

"I'm sure everything will be fine." He looked at his watch and said, "We should probably get upstairs."

Though he had resigned himself to the idea of her being the surrogate and had for the most part convinced himself it was for the best, deep down he half hoped the doctor would find some reason to deem her an inappropriate candidate for the procedure. But after a thorough examination, Katy was given a clean bill of health. And like her own physician, Dr. Meyer even went so far as to comment that her body was ideal for childbearing. So there was definitely no turning back now.

It was a done deal.

After a consultation with the doctor in his office, where he explained the procedure in great detail, they made an appointment for the following week to have two embryos implanted.

"Are you nervous?" Katy asked him as they walked back down to the lobby together.

He shrugged.

"Oh, come on, you have to be at least a little nervous."

"I guess." After waiting so long for this, the process did seem to be moving very quickly. "How about you? Are you having second thoughts?"

"Not at all. I'm just really excited. I can hardly believe it's next week. I thought it would take months."

"It won't be a problem, you leaving the ranch for a couple of days?"

"They can get by without me. But I was thinking, because I'll be on bed rest for twenty-four hours after the transfer, maybe you could recommend a hotel."

Did she honestly think he would let her stay alone in a hotel? Not only would that be rude and insensitive of him, he wanted her close by, so he could keep an eye on her and make sure she followed the doctor's orders to the letter. They had three shots at this. He didn't want anything going wrong.

"Nonsense," he told her. "You'll stay with me."

"Are you sure? I don't want to impose."

They pushed out the door into the blazing afternoon heat where his car sat at the curb already waiting for him. "Of course I'm sure."

"In that case, thanks. It's been years since I've been to your house."

Three years to be exact. The day of Becca's funeral.

They stopped on the sidewalk near the limo. He really should get back to work, but she'd driven all this way and the least he could do was feed her.

"Why don't I buy you lunch?"

"I really need to get going," she said apologetically. "I'll probably just swing into the drive-through on my way home."

She would decline his invitation for something as unpalatable as fast food? Not to mention unhealthy. "Are you sure? There's a café just around the corner."

"I promised my folks I would make a few stops for them on the way home, and I don't want to get back too late. Can I take a rain check?"

"Of course," he said, though her casual refusal puzzled him. When it came to women, he was usually the one declining offers. And lately there had been plenty of them, no thanks to one of his coworkers who thought Adam had done enough grieving and needed to get back into circulation.

Not that Adam considered Katy a woman. In the relationship sense, that is. In his eyes she was a business associate. One who was looking at him curiously.

"What?"

"If it means that much to you, we can go," she said.

"Go?"

"To lunch. You looked...I don't know...disappointed."

Had he? "No, of course not."

"You're sure? Because I can make the time."

"Of course I'm sure."

She didn't look as though she believed him. "I know this has to be tough for you. I mean, as much as you want a child, they're Becca's eggs. It must stir up a lot of feelings." She took a step toward him, reached out and put a hand on his arm. Why did she have to do that? Be so...physical? "If you need someone to talk to—"

"I don't," he assured her, his gaze straying

to her cleavage. Probably because there was so much of it, and she was standing so close that it was right there, inches from his face. Okay, more than inches, but still.

"Hello!" she said, snapping her fingers in front of his eyes, until he lifted them to hers. "I'm trying to be nice, and all you can do is stare at my boobs? And people wonder why I dress the way I do."

She was right. That was totally inappropriate. He was acting like he'd never seen breasts before. When not only had he seen breasts, he'd seen hers.

"I apologize," he said, keeping his eyes on her face. "And no, I don't need to talk."

"I just figured you asked me to lunch for a reason."

"I did. I thought you might be hungry."

She sighed heavily. "Okay. But I'm here if you change your mind. Just call me."

"I won't."

"You know, it wouldn't kill you to lighten up a little. You're so serious all the time. That can't be healthy."

"You've never seen me at work. I'm a party animal."

She rolled her eyes. "Sure you are."

"So I'll see you next week?" he asked, anxious to end this nightmare of a conversation. She seemed to have an annoying way of getting under his skin.

"See you next week."

She turned and sashayed to her truck, hips swaying, curls bouncing. Anyone looking at her would know, just from the way she walked, that she had attitude.

And suddenly he was picturing her naked again. Wondering what she would have done if he'd stepped into her room, if he had reached for her…

"Sir?" Reece said, and Adam realized he was standing there holding the door open, and he'd heard their entire exchange. "She's something, huh?"

She was *something* all right. He just hadn't quite figured out what.

"She's really quite beautiful, isn't she?"

"I guess."

Reece didn't say a word, but his expression

said he knew his boss was full of it. That any red-blooded heterosexual male would have to be blind not to think she was totally hot. But the last thing Adam needed was for his driver to think he had a thing for his surrogate. Not that he didn't trust Reece implicitly, but there were certain lines a man did not cross, even hypothetically.

This was definitely one of them.

Katy assumed the week would crawl by, but before she knew it, she was on her way back to El Paso. Adam had called a few days earlier, suggesting she come to stay the night before, so she wouldn't have to make the two-hour drive before the appointment, but she told him no. As nervous and excited as she knew she would be, sleeping would be tough enough without being in an unfamiliar room, in a strange bed. And for some reason, the thought of sleeping in the same house with Adam made her nervous. Not that she thought he would try something. It just felt…weird. But tonight she didn't have a choice. She physically couldn't drive home.

Her mother had offered to drive her to El Paso and stay for the procedure, then drive her directly back. She wasn't too keen on Katy staying at Adam's place, either. But the doctor said bed rest, and she couldn't exactly sack out in the truck bed for the two-hour drive.

Adam still lived in the sprawling, six-bedroom, seven-bath, eight-thousand-square-foot monstrosity Becca had insisted they needed. They could have had a whole brood of children and still had space to spare. And though she loved her sister dearly, and was sure that she had been a very accomplished interior designer, her personal tastes were excessive to say the least, and bordering on gaudy. She didn't seem to understand the concept of less is more.

Katy pulled up the circle drive and parked by the front door, next to the concrete, cherub-adorned fountain, realizing how utterly out of place her truck looked there.

She grabbed her duffel from the front seat, climbed out and walked to the front entrance, but before she could ring the bell the door swung open. Standing there was Adam's housekeeper, whom Katy vaguely remembered from the day of Becca's funeral, an older woman with a gently lined and kind face.

Though Adam seemed the type to insist his staff wear a formal uniform, she was dressed in jeans and a Texas A & M sweatshirt.

She smiled warmly. "Ms. Huntley, so nice to see you again! I'm Celia."

Katy liked her immediately.

"Hi, Celia."

"Come in, come in!" She ushered Katy inside, taking the bag before she could protest. The air was filled with the scent of something warm and sweet. "Can you believe how hot it is and it's barely 10:00 a.m.? Why don't I show you to your room, then I'll get you something cold to drink. Are you hungry? I could fix you breakfast."

"I'm fine, thanks." She'd been too nervous to force down more than a slice of toast and a glass of juice before she left home. "Is Adam here?"

"He went into the office for a few hours. He's sending a car for you at ten-thirty."

She'd been under the impression they would ride to the appointment together, but she should have known he would squeeze in a few hours at the office first. Hadn't that always been Becca's biggest complaint? That Adam worked too much. Which begged the question, when would he have time to take care of a baby? But it was a little late to worry about that now.

Celia led Katy across the foyer and either Katy had a skewed recollection of the interior, or Adam had made changes to the decor because it wasn't nearly as distasteful as she remembered. Considering she had only been here twice before, it was difficult to be sure. In any case, it was very warm and inviting now.

They walked up to the second floor and Celia showed her to one of the spare bedrooms. If Katy was remembering right, the master was at the end of the hall not twenty feet away. She didn't like that Adam would be in such close proximity, but what could she do, ask to sack out on the living-room couch? At least Celia would be there to act as a buffer.

Besides, she was being silly. She was only staying there because it was convenient. And because, she suspected, Adam didn't completely trust her to follow the doctor's instructions, if left to her own devices. She had to admit that being flat on her back for twenty-four hours sounded like the worst kind of torture. She was not an idle person.

She didn't have the patience to sit around doing nothing. But this time she didn't have a choice.

"This is nice," Katy said, looking around as Celia set her bag down on the floral duvet. The room was tastefully decorated in creamy pastels. Feminine and inviting without being too frilly.

"There are fresh towels in the bathroom. And if you need anything, anything at all while you're here, don't hesitate to ask. I think it's a very generous thing you're doing for Adam. Since he decided to do this, it's the happiest I've seen him since he lost Becca. He would deny it if you asked, but the last few years have been very hard on him. I was starting to believe he would never get over her."

If he loved her that much, why did Becca have to work so hard to keep him happy? she wanted to ask. Why was she always terrified that he would grow bored and leave her for someone else? Maybe Celia wasn't seeing the whole picture, or hadn't known Adam long enough to realize what he was really like.

Katy sat on the edge of the bed. "How long have you worked for Adam?"

"Ever since his father passed. But I've known

him most of his life. I practically raised him. When he wasn't off at boarding school, that is."

"Oh, I didn't realize you'd been with the family that long."

"Going on thirty-two years now. Since Mrs. Blair, Adam's mother, took ill. I lost my own boy in the Gulf War, so Adam has been like a son to me."

"I'm so sorry," Katy said. Losing a child was a sorrow her parents knew all too well.

"I still consider myself blessed. I have two beautiful daughters and five grandchildren between them."

"What do you think of Adam having a child? If you don't mind my asking."

Celia sat down beside her. "I think Adam will be a wonderful father. He lets my grandchildren come over and use the pool, and he's so good with them. He's wanted this for a very long time."

Celia was probably biased, but Katy wanted desperately to believe her. Although, wanting a child, and being good with someone else's grandchildren, didn't necessarily make someone a good parent.

"When you get to know him better, you'll see," Celia assured her.

"But how am I supposed to get to know him when he's so closed off. So uptight."

"That's just a smokescreen. Though he doesn't let it show, he feels very deeply. He's been hurt, Katy. It takes him time to trust. But he's a good man." She laid a hand on Katy's knee. "I know it's been hard for you and your parents. And probably nothing I can say will totally reassure you. But I promise you, Adam would never do anything to deliberately hurt anyone. Especially family."

"I want to believe that." But she didn't. Not for a second. Because that would mean everything her sister had told her was a lie. And believing that wasn't an option.

Six

On a normal day, Adam was an active participant at the informal weekly management team briefing they held in his office, but today he couldn't stop looking at the clock.

Nathaniel Everett, their Chief Brand Officer was explaining the new campaign his team had been developing to promote their latest, ecologically friendly practices. Groundbreaking upgrades that would not only keep them in line with future federal guidelines, but no doubt result in record profits.

On a normal day that would have filled Adam with a thrilling sense of accomplishment, but today his heart just wasn't in it. In fact, for a while now, six months at least, work didn't hold the same appeal as it had in the past. And that fact hadn't escaped his team.

At first he'd written it off as a temporary slump, but when he didn't go back to feeling like his old self, he began to suspect it was something deeper. Clearly something was missing. There was a void in his life, in his very soul that work would no longer fill. It was when he knew it was time to have a child.

"So, what do you think?" he heard Nathan ask, and realized he had completely zoned out.

"Good," he said, hoping he could fake his way through.

Nathan smiled wryly. "You haven't heard a damn thing I've said, have you?"

He could lie, but what was the point? "Sorry. I'm off my game today."

"Rough night?" Nathan's brother, Jordan, their Chief Operations Officer, asked, his tone suggestive. He'd been asserting for months that Adam's major problem was he needed to get laid. And while Adam wouldn't deny he'd been...*tense* lately, random sex with a woman he barely knew was Jordan's thing, not his. In fact, common knowledge of Jordan's sexual prowess was what had endeared him to the roughnecks on the rig. Despite his Ivy League education, they related to him somehow. Looked up to him even. He managed to fit in, yet still hold his own in the boardroom without batting an eye. He was like a chameleon, changing color to suit his environment.

Adam envied him that sometimes.

"Only because I didn't sleep well," he told Jordan. "Maybe we can reschedule for tomorrow."

Jordan shrugged. "Fine by me."

"I have a meeting with Cassandra anyway," Nathan told him, rising from his chair. "Should we say 10:00 a.m.?"

Everyone agreed, then gathered their things and left. Emilio, who had been quiet through most of the meeting, hung back.

"Everything all right?" he asked. He obviously didn't buy that a simple lack of sleep could leave Adam so distracted.

"Katy and I have an appointment today. In fact, I have to leave soon or I'm going to be late."

"The fertility doctor?" he asked.

Adam nodded. "She's having the embryos transferred today."

"I didn't realize it would be so soon. Congratulations."

"That doesn't mean it will work, but Katy is young and healthy and the doctor seems hopeful."

"I'll keep my fingers crossed for you. I guess I don't have to ask if you're nervous."

It took a lot to set him on edge, but today the pressure was getting to him. "It shows, huh?"

"Hey, who wouldn't be? This is a big step you're taking."

Adam looked at his watch. "And I have to meet Katy."

Emilio turned to leave, but stopped in the doorway. "I meant to ask the other day. This is probably none of my business.…"

"What?"

"Well, since Becca had cancer, and that can be genetic…I just wondered if that would put your child at risk. It runs in my family, too. On my father's side."

"I've spoken to a geneticist and the fact that

cervical cancer doesn't run in either of our families reduces the risk of predisposing the baby."

Emilio grinned. "So you've done your research. That's what I figured. Well, good luck."

When he was gone Adam grabbed what he needed and headed down to the parking garage. Since Reece had gone to get Katy, he took the company limo to the doctor's office. When he got inside, she was already there in the lobby waiting for him. And this time he had no trouble spotting her. She stood by the elevator bank, her face flush with excitement, dressed in her "girl" clothes again. This time it was a yellow sundress with a fitted bodice and A-line skirt, and instead of boots she'd worn strappy, flat-soled sandals.

Though he would never admit it to anyone, she looked sexy as hell. And if she were anyone but his sister-in-law, or his surrogate, he just might put an end to his three-year dating freeze and ask her out to dinner.

But no matter how attractive he found her, she was who she was, which kept her strictly off-limits. Not that she would agree to go out with him if he did ask. Knowing her, she would refuse on principle alone, just to irritate him.

"Early again, I see," he said as he approached her.

"You can thank Reece for that. He was worried about traffic."

He stabbed the button for the second floor. "Did you get settled in at the house?"

"I did, and Celia seems wonderful."

"She is."

"She really adores you, you know. You're lucky to have someone like that in your life."

She didn't have to tell him that. After his mother died, and his father took a permanent emotional vacation, Celia was the only "parent" he'd had. She wasn't just his housekeeper. She was family. He couldn't imagine what his life would be like now if it hadn't been for her.

"How can you look so calm?" she asked as the doors slid open and they stepped in. "I don't think I've ever been so nervous in my life."

"I don't do nervous." Katy must have put on perfume, too, because she smelled really nice. Flowery and feminine, but not overpoweringly so. In fact, the scent was so faint, yet so intoxicating, he had the urge to lean in closer and breathe her in. Bury his nose in the silky curls tumbling like silk ribbons across her shoulders.

Silk ribbons? Jesus, he needed to get his head examined.

"How could you not be nervous?" she said, clearly unwilling to let the subject drop.

"Okay, I'm a little nervous. Happy?"

"Well, if you are, you sure don't look it. I guess you're just really good at hiding your feelings."

"That comes as part of the outdoor plumbing package." The doors slid open and they stepped out, but when he turned to Katy she had a funny look on her face. "What?"

"Did you just make a joke?"

"I guess so. Is that a problem?"

"The ability to joke suggests you have a sense of humor. Adam, I had no idea."

He tried to looked indignant, but the corners of his mouth twitched upward.

She gasped. "Oh, my gosh! You just smiled! Do you know that since I met you at Western Oil that day I haven't seen you smile a single time? I didn't even realize you still knew how."

In spite of himself, he smiled wider. "All right, you've made your point."

She gave him a playful poke. "Better be careful, or God forbid, people might start to think you have feelings."

What she didn't realize was that he felt very deeply. Too much for his own good, in fact. And look where it had gotten him.

Which is why he expended so much effort to feel as little as possible now. Or at the very least, not let it show.

They walked down the hall to the fertility suite and were immediately shown into the doctor's private office for a quick consultation, in case they had any last-minute questions—a courtesy Adam was sure he reserved for only his special patients. In other words, the ones with the thickest wallets. Dr. Meyer had a fund for lower-income couples with medical conditions preventing them from conceiving, and understanding their pain, not to mention the perks it would include, Adam had donated generously.

After a brief chat, they were taken to the room where Katy would change into her gown.

"I guess this is it," Adam said. "I'll see you afterward."

"Afterward?" she asked, looking confused.

"You're not going to come in for the procedure. I thought you would want to be there."

"I do. I just...I thought it would make you uncomfortable."

"Call me old-fashioned, but I believe a father should at least be in the room when his child is conceived. Even if he's not actually...you know... doing the work."

Leave it to Katy to be absolutely blunt. "If you're comfortable with it, then sure, count me in."

"The doctor knows the situation. I'm sure he can be discreet. And if not..." she shrugged. "It's not like you haven't seen me naked. And you'll be seeing it all again when the baby is born. Right?"

He had hoped she would allow him to be in the delivery room, but he figured he would wait until later in the pregnancy to ask. Now he didn't have to worry.

He didn't doubt that if he'd hired a surrogate, a stranger, she might not be as open to him being so involved in the entire process. And he appreciated it. More than Katy would ever know.

"Well, I better go change," she said. "Don't want to keep the embryos waiting."

"Thank you, Katy."

She smiled, then she did something totally unexpected. She rose up on her toes and pressed a kiss to his cheek.

Her lips were soft and warm and just the slightest bit damp. And though it didn't last long, just a second or two, something happened. Something passed between them, although he couldn't say for sure what it was. If it was physical or emotional. But whatever it was, he felt it straight through to his bones. And clearly, so did she.

She stepped back, looking puzzled, lifting a hand up to touch her lips. And something must have been wrong with him because his first instinct was to take her in his arms and draw her against him, bury his face against her hair and just…hold her. He wondered what she would do if he tried.

But he didn't, and after a few seconds the moment, whatever it was, seemed to pass.

"I guess I better go," she said, glancing back to the nurse who was waiting for her, looking apprehensive, as if the gravity of what she was about to do had suddenly taken hold. "You'll be there?"

Maybe she just didn't want to feel as though she was in this alone. "I'll be there," he assured her, and realized that his heart was beating faster. Maybe he was more nervous than he'd thought. Or could it have been something else?

She started to turn, and before he realized what he was doing, he reached out and grabbed her arm. Startled, she turned back to him, looking at his hand as though she was surprised he would touch her. And honestly, he was a bit surprised himself.

"You're sure you want to do this," he said. "It's not too late to back out."

The apprehension seemed to dissolve before his eyes and she smiled. A really sweet, pretty smile that he was sure he would remember for the rest of his life.

"I'm sure," she said, placing her hand over his. "I want to do this."

He let his hand slip out from under hers and fall to his side.

"You can sit in the procedure waiting room," the nurse said, pointing it out to him. "They'll call you in when she's ready."

The waiting room was blessedly empty, but

after twenty minutes passed he began to worry they had forgotten about him. He was about to get up and ask someone what was taking so long when another nurse appeared in the doorway. She led him to an exam room where Katy was already in position with her feet in the stirrups, ready to go. And other than a bit of bare leg, she was very discreetly covered.

She looked relieved to see him.

"Is everyone ready?" the doctor asked, looking from Katy to Adam.

Adam nodded. Katy took a deep breath, exhaled and said, "Let's do it."

She reached for his hand and he took it, holding firmly as the doctor did the transfer. The procedure itself seemed pretty simple, and if Katy's occasional winces were any indication, involved only minor discomfort. Within ten minutes it was over.

"That's it," Dr. Meyer said, peeling off his gloves. "Now comes the hard part. The waiting."

Per his orders Katy had to lie there for two hours before she would be allowed home, so after the staff cleared the room Adam pulled a chair up beside her and sat down.

"I think it worked," she said, looking content-edly serene. "I can almost feel the cells beginning to divide."

"Is that even possible?" he asked.

She shrugged. "Probably not, but I have a good feeling about this."

He didn't want to get his hopes up, but he had a good feeling about it, too. Something about the day, the entire experience felt...special. Like it was meant to be. Which was strange, since he'd never been superstitious.

She looked over at him and smiled. "If someone had told me a month ago that I would be here today, having fertilized embryos injected into me, I would have told them they were insane."

Boy, could he relate. He always knew that someday he would use the embryos, but not with Katy as the surrogate. "If it's unsuccessful, are you still willing to try again?"

"Of course! I'm in this for the long haul." She yawned deeply, her eyes overflowing with tears. "Well, goodness, all of the sudden I feel exhausted."

She must have slept as fitfully as he had last

night. Plus she'd had that long drive this morning. "Why don't you close your eyes and rest."

"Maybe just for a minute," she said, her eyes slipping closed. Within minutes her breathing became slow and deep and her lips parted slightly. He sat there looking at her and had the strangest urge to touch her face. To run his finger across her full bottom lip...

He shook away the thought. He hoped this was a one-shot deal. He hoped the test came up positive, not only because he wanted a child, but because he wanted to get the emotionally taxing part of the process out of the way. This entire experience was doing strange things to his head.

He sat there for a while, checking messages and reading email on his phone. Then he played a few games of Tetris.

After an hour, when she was still out cold, he decided to make a few calls. Careful not to disturb her, he stepped out into the hall and called Celia on his cell, asking her to have lunch ready when they got back, then he checked in with his secretary and returned a few other calls that couldn't wait until he got back to the office.

When he finally returned to the room, Katy was awake.

"Oh, there you are," she said, looking anxious. "I thought maybe you'd left."

Did she really think he would just up and leave her there alone? "Of course not. I just had a few calls to make and I didn't want to disturb you." He reclaimed his seat. "Did you have a good nap?"

"Yeah. I must have gone out cold. All the stress probably. At least now, if we have to do it again, I'll know what to expect." She touched his arm. "I wish it could have been Becca here with you."

Emotion caught in his throat. "Me, too."

There was a knock at the door, then the nurse stuck her head in. "You can get dressed and go now."

"Already? I guess I slept longer than I thought."

"And don't forget, strict bed rest for the next twenty-four hours," she said sternly.

"Like I could forget that," she muttered, sitting up.

Adam waited in the hall while Katy put her clothes on, then they went to the reception desk to make an appointment for her blood test in ten days.

"Can you believe that ten days from now we'll know if I'm pregnant?" she said excitedly as they walked down to the limo. His only concern right now was getting her home and back into bed. Although he was sure, the next ten days might just be the longest of his life.

Seven

It was official. Katy was starting to dislike Adam a lot less.

She had just assumed that when they got back to his place he would get her settled, pat her on the head and say good job, then motor off to the office for a shareholders meeting or something equally important sounding. In reality, he had barely left her side all day. She watched television and Adam sat in a chair beside the bed with his laptop.

He must have asked her a hundred times if there was anything she needed, anything he could do for her. And here she had honestly believed the only person he cared about was himself. He'd even smiled a few times.

And that kiss back in the doctor's office? What was up with that? It had been an impulse on her part. After all, what they were doing was pretty personal. It just seemed like the right thing to do. She'd never expected to *feel* it. Although to be honest she still wasn't sure what it was exactly that she'd felt. It was an odd sort of…awareness. Not sexual exactly, but not completely innocent, either. It was as if some deeper part of each of them had risen to the surface and collided, causing a sort of cosmic friction or interference or something. And she could tell, by the look on Adam's face, that he'd felt it, too.

It had been a weird, but not unpleasant experience. In fact, it felt sort of nice. But that didn't mean she wanted it to happen again. Unfortunately the more she tried to forget it, forget how smooth his cheek felt, the tangy scent of his aftershave, the more it consumed her.

She couldn't help sneaking looks his way, wondering if he was thinking about it, too. But she wasn't being as sneaky as she thought because he finally looked over at her and asked, "Is there a reason you keep looking at me?"

"Am I?" she asked, as if she'd had no clue. "I didn't realize. I guess I must be doing it unconsciously."

"Okay," he said, although he didn't look as though he believed her. But he didn't push the issue, either. And she was glad. She made a conscious effort not to look at him again.

Around six when Celia brought them supper on a tray, it was a relief to be able to sit up for a while. Celia set her tray over her lap, then gestured Adam to the opposite side of the bed.

"You, sit," she ordered.

"I am sitting."

"Now, *niño pequeño,*" she said sternly. "Little Boy." A holdover nickname from when he was small, Katy was guessing.

"Why can't I eat here?" He sounded like a little boy arguing with his mother.

"Because I said so, that's why. Now move, before your supper gets cold."

"You're seriously not going to let me eat here? In a chair, I might add, that I *own?*"

"And you honestly think I'm going to let you

eat spaghetti on *Persian silk?* Becca would roll over in her grave."

He seemed to get that it was a losing battle, because he shoved himself up from the chair and mumbled, "The way you boss me around, a person would think this was your house."

He rounded the bed, kicked off his shoes and climbed on, sitting cross-legged next to Katy. "Happy now?"

"Good boy," Celia said, setting his tray in front of him, stopping just shy of patting his head. He looked more than a little annoyed, which Katy was guessing was the whole point. He may have *owned* the house, but Celia was clearly in charge.

It was one of the sweetest, most heartwarming things she had ever seen. The big powerful billionaire was really just a pussycat.

"Can I get you anything else?" Celia asked.

"A double scotch if it wouldn't be too much trouble," Adam said.

She smiled and said, "Of course. Katy?"

"Under the circumstances, I should probably lay off the booze. But thanks for asking."

"I didn't mean…" She sighed and shook her

head, as if they were both hopeless. "Heaven help us, you're just as bad as he is."

She walked out mumbling to herself.

"Niño pequeño?" Katy asked, unable to stifle a smile.

"I swear sometimes she thinks I'm still ten years old," he grumbled, but there was affection in his eyes. He loved Celia, even if he didn't want to admit it.

"I think everyone needs someone to boss them around every once in a while," she said. "It keeps you grounded."

"Well, then, I should be pretty well-grounded, because she bosses me around on a daily basis."

And she could tell that though he wanted Katy to believe otherwise, he wouldn't have it any other way.

Celia returned several minutes later with his drink, then left them to eat. Katy just assumed that when they were finished, Adam would sit in the chair again. Instead he fluffed the pillows and leaned back against them. It was probably the most laid-back she had ever seen him. In fact, she'd never imagined he could be so relaxed.

She couldn't help but wonder if it had anything

to do with the scotch. Maybe the alcohol had lowered his inhibitions. She recalled Becca telling her once, a long time ago, that if she wanted something, all she had to do was give him a drink or two and he was about as staunch as a wet noodle. And while Katy didn't necessarily believe it was ethical to take advantage of an intoxicated person, if it made him open up to her a little…well, what was the harm?

When Celia came back for their dishes, Katy asked her for a glass of orange juice. "And I think Adam could use another drink."

He looked at his watch, then shrugged and said, "Why not?"

Around nine, after he'd drained his second glass and was clearly feeling no pain—he'd even laughed during one of the shows—she used the bathroom and changed into her pajamas, then climbed back into bed. The program they'd been watching had just ended, so she switched off the television, rolled on her side to face him and asked, "Adam, can we talk?"

He looked down at her and frowned. "Is something wrong?"

"Oh, no, nothing," she assured him. "It just only

seems right that I should get to know the father of the baby I'll be carrying. Don't you think?"

His brow dipped low. "Oh, you mean you want to *talk*."

"What have you got against talking? It's how people get to know each other."

He looked uncomfortable. "That wasn't part of the deal."

"Maybe it should be."

"You know, my life isn't really all that interesting."

"I doubt that." She gave him a playful poke. "Come on, tell me something about you. Just one thing."

"Let me think. Oh, I know. I don't like talking about myself."

She laughed. "Adam!"

"What?" he said with a grin. "You said one thing."

"Something I don't already know. Tell me about…your father."

He shrugged. "There isn't much to tell."

"Were you close?"

"There were times, when my mom was still alive, that he would occasionally notice me. But then she died, and he checked out."

That was the saddest thing she'd ever heard. If they were all the other had, they should have stuck together. They could have leaned on each other. The way she and her parents supported each other when Becca died. She supposed that sort of tragedy could either pull a family together, or rip them apart.

"You must have been very lonely."

He shrugged again, "Celia was there for me."

He said it so casually, but she had the feeling that losing his mother had scarred him deeper than he would ever admit. How could it not?

"How did your mother die?"

"Cancer."

Which must have made learning about Becca's cancer all the more devastating. And scary. "How old were you?"

"Young enough to believe it was my fault."

She sucked in a quiet breath. That was probably the most honest thing he had ever said to her. Her heart ached for him. For the frightened little boy he must have been.

He looked over at her. "Everyone has bad things happen to them, Katy. You get through it, you move on."

Was he forgetting that she had lost someone dear to her, too?

"Have you?" she asked. "Moved on, I mean." She knew the instant the words were out, as the shutters on his emotions snapped closed again, that she had pushed too far. So much for getting to know one another.

He looked at his watch and frowned. "It's getting late."

He got up and grabbed his shoes from the floor.

"You don't have to go," she said. "We can talk about something else."

His expression said he'd had just about all the conversation he could stand for one night. Maybe a dozen nights. Maybe he was only in here to keep tabs on her. To be sure that she followed the doctor's instructions. "You need your rest and I have an early meeting tomorrow. I probably won't see you in the morning, but Celia will get you whatever you need."

Like the turtles she and Willy used to catch in the grass by the riverbank when she was a kid, he'd sensed danger and retreated back into his shell. God forbid he let himself open up to her, let himself *feel* something. Would it really be so terrible?

He hesitated in the doorway, like he might change his mind, but instead he said, "Have a safe trip back to Peckins," then he was gone.

Adam had actually started acting like a human being today, which she couldn't deny intrigued her. And now that she'd had a preview of the man hiding behind the icy exterior, she wanted to dig deeper. She wanted to know who he was.

But when had this ever been about getting to know Adam better? And why would she bother? When it was over, and the baby was born, they would just go back to being strangers. Seeing each other occasionally when he brought the baby around.

She laid a hand gently across her belly, wondering what was going on inside, if the procedure had worked and the embryo was attaching to her womb. Her tiny little niece or nephew, she thought with a smile. Even knowing that there was only an average 10 percent success rate, she had a good feeling about their chances.

She switched off the light and lay in the dark, thinking about everything that had happened since she left Peckins that morning. The ease of the procedure, and the way Adam had stayed with her all day. She thought that they had shared something special, that they were becoming friends, but it was clear he didn't want that. And for some stupid reason the idea made her inexplicably sad.

It had only been seven days since the procedure, and would be three more days before she would even know if she was pregnant, and Katy had already determined that she agreed to have a child with the most demanding and obstinate man on the face of the earth.

Adam had called her about a *million* times.

Okay, so it was more like fifteen or twenty, but it sure felt like a million. She had only been back to Peckins an hour when he phoned to check on her, which, in light of his cool attitude the night before, she found sort of touching. He reminded her that the doctor said to take it easy for several days, meaning no heavy lifting or strenuous activity. Which she, of course, already knew. She assured him she was following the postprocedure instructions to the letter, and he had nothing to worry about.

Thinking that she'd made herself pretty clear, she was surprised when later that evening he'd called *again.*

Was she eating right? Drinking enough water? Staying off her feet?

She patiently assured him that she was *still* following the doctor's orders, and when they hung up shortly after, assumed that would be the last she heard from him in a while. But he called again the next morning.

Had she gotten a full eight hours sleep? She wasn't drinking coffee, was she? And since country breakfasts were often laden with saturated fats, she should consider fruit and an egg-white omelet as a substitute.

She assured him again, maybe not quite so patiently this time, that she knew what to do. And she was only a little surprised when he called later in the day to say he'd been doing research on the internet and needed her email address so he could send her links to several sites he thought contained necessary information about prenatal health. And had she ever considered becoming a vegetarian?

If he was this fanatical before there was even a confirmed pregnancy, what was he going to be like when she was actually pregnant? Two to three calls a day, *every* day, for nine months?

She would be giving birth from a padded room in the psychiatric ward.

It wouldn't be so bad if the phone calls were even slightly conversational in tone. As in, "Hi, how are you? What have you been up to?" Instead he more or less barked orders, without even the most basic of pleasantries.

On day seven, he called to say that he'd been giving their situation considerable thought, and he'd come to the conclusion that he would feel more comfortable if she came to stay with him in El Paso for the duration of her pregnancy. So he could "keep a close eye on her."

It was the final straw.

"I will not, under any circumstances, drop everything and move two hours from home. The ranch is my life. My parents need me here. And all the phone calls and emails…it has to stop.

You're *smothering* me and we don't even know that I'm pregnant yet."

"But you could be, so doesn't it make sense to start taking care of yourself now? This is my child we're talking about."

"It's also my life."

"If you were here with me I wouldn't have to call. And you wouldn't have to do anything. Celia would take care of you."

She liked Celia, but honestly, it sounded like hell on earth. She wasn't an idle person. Most days she was up before dawn and didn't stop moving until bedtime. "I *love* working, Adam."

"But obviously you'll have to quit."

"Why would I do that?"

"Because you'll be pregnant."

Oh, he did *not* just say that. "What century are you living in? Pregnant women work all the time."

"At a desk job maybe, or as a clerk in a store. I seriously doubt there are pregnant women out there roping cattle on horseback and mucking stables."

"Is *that* what you think I do?"

"It's not?"

"Not *just* that. And, of course, I wouldn't do those things when I'm pregnant. Do you really think I would be that irresponsible? And for your information, I spend a *lot* of time behind a desk."

"I didn't mean to imply that you're irresponsible. And I guess I just assumed your responsibilities were more physical in nature."

"So you assumed I got a business degree just for the fun of it?" she snapped. "Next you'll be telling me that I'm wasting my education staying on the ranch." As if she hadn't heard that enough from Becca over the years.

"I'm just worried about the health of my child."

"We obviously need to get a few things straight here. One, I am *not* moving to El Paso. There is no reason why I can't have a perfectly healthy pregnancy in Peckins. And two, I am definitely not quitting work. My parents depend on me, not to mention that I love what I do. I understand that you're worried about the baby's health, but you're just going to have to trust me. And lastly, if you insist on calling to check up on me, could you have the decency to not treat me like a…a *baby factory.* Maybe we could even have a conversation. You do know what that is, right?"

"Yes," he said curtly. He obviously didn't like what he was hearing, but when she signed the contract to be his surrogate, nowhere did it say she had to comply to his every demand.

Move in with him? Was he nuts?

"Even though Becca is gone, we're still family. Would it really be so terrible if we were friends?"

"I never said I didn't want to be your friend."

"You didn't have to. I'm sure you've heard the phrase, *actions speak louder than words*. And maybe you haven't considered this, but if you get to know me a little better, it will be easier for you to trust me."

"I suppose you're right," he said grudgingly.

At least it was start. But she had the sinking feeling that it was going to a really *long* nine months.

<u>Eight</u>

Since their phone conversation three days ago, Adam had cut off all contact with Katy, and it had been surprisingly difficult. Since the procedure he'd been thinking about her almost twenty-four/seven. The more he read up on pregnancy, the deeper home it hit just how many things could go wrong with not just the baby, but Katy, as well.

He had accepted responsibility for Becca's death, and learned to live with the guilt, but the idea that her sister's life was now in his hands had him on constant edge. It was his responsibility to make sure she was healthy.

It was something he should have considered

before he put this baby plan into motion. But it was too late now. Katie was due to arrive any minute so they could go for her blood test. In a few hours they would know if the procedure worked.

He was both excited and dreading it. Hopeful but conflicted. From his home office, where he'd been working while waiting for her to arrive, he heard the doorbell. Even though he was sure it was Katy, he let Celia answer it.

After a minute, Celia knocked on his door. "Katy is here, and I think something is wrong. She ran straight upstairs to the spare bedroom. And it looked like she'd been crying."

He bolted up from his chair, his heart in the pit of his stomach.

With Celia close behind Adam rushed up the stairs to the spare room. The door was open, so he stepped inside. The door to the bathroom was closed. He knocked softly and asked, "Katy, are you all right?"

"Give me a minute," she called.

He walked back over to the bedroom door to wait with Celia. After several minutes the bathroom door opened and Katy emerged. She was in her girls' clothes, and her red-rimmed eyes said she probably had been crying.

Ridiculous as it was, his first instinct was to take her in his arms and try to comfort her, which was exactly why he didn't.

"What's wrong?" he asked.

"I had some light cramping this morning before I left, but I thought it might just be a fluke." She sniffled and swiped at the tear that had spilled over onto her cheek. "But it wasn't."

The disappointment was all-encompassing. "You're not pregnant?"

She bit her lip and shook her head. "I was so sure it worked. I really expected to be pregnant."

Celia crossed the room and gathered Katy in her arms, and Adam couldn't help thinking that it should be him comforting her. But he was glad Celia had stepped in for him.

"You'll have more chances," Celia assured her, rubbing her back soothingly. "I know it's disappointing, but it will happen." She looked over at Adam and gestured to the box of tissue on the nightstand.

He plucked one out and brought it to her. Celia took it and pressed it into Katy's hand.

"Why don't I make you a soothing cup of chamomile tea?"

Katy sniffled and nodded.

Celia turned and gave Adam a look, then jerked her head in Katy's direction, as if to say "Console her, you idiot." But he couldn't seem to make himself do it.

Katy stood there dabbing her eyes. "I was so sure I was pregnant."

"The doctor said it could take a few times."

"I know, but I had such a good feeling." She took a deep, shuddering breath. "I'm so sorry, Adam."

"Sorry for what?"

"I feel responsible."

She looked so damned…forlorn. And Katy never struck him as the kind of woman to cry on a whim. He recalled that even at Becca's funeral she'd held it together. And how could he just stand there, like a selfish bastard, when he was the one who put her in this situation? Had he really grown so cold and unfeeling?

Or was it that he felt *too* much?

"I'm sorry," she said in a wobbly voice. "I'm acting stupid."

Another tear spilled over and rolled down her cheek, and he cringed. The gene all men possessed that made them wither at the sight of a crying female kicked into overdrive. Besides, if he didn't do something, she would probably just interpret it as him being mad at her, or something equally ridiculous.

Feeling he had no choice, he stepped closer and tugged her into his arms. She came willingly, leaning into the embrace, hands fisted against his chest, head tucked under his chin.

There it was again, just like when she'd kissed his cheek, that feeling of awareness. As if every touch, every sensation was multiplied tenfold. The softness of her body where it pressed against his. The flowery scent of her hair. The flutter of her breath through his shirt and the warmth that seemed to seep through her clothing to his skin.

His body began to react the way any man's would. Well, any man who hadn't been this physically close to a woman in three years. Or intimate in closer to four. Until recently he couldn't say he'd missed it. He'd barely given any thought to sex. It was as if his body had been in deep hibernation, unable to feel physical pleasure.

But he sure as hell could feel it now. And if he didn't get a hold of himself, she would feel it, too.

"I'm sorry," she said again.

"Would you *stop* apologizing."

"I just feel like, maybe if I had done something different, if I had been more careful."

Beating herself up over this wasn't going to change anything. "It was nothing you did."

"But you only have embryos for two more attempts. What if those fail, too?"

"I knew going into this that there was a chance it wouldn't work. I do have other options."

"But then the last of Becca will be gone forever."

"Katy, look at me." She didn't move, so he cradled her chin in his palm and lifted her face to his. Big mistake. Her eyes were wide and sad, and so blue he could almost swim in their depths, and when they locked on his, the sensation was so intense he felt it like a physical blow. Whatever it was he'd been about to say to her was lost.

Her lips parted, like she might speak, and his eyes were drawn to her mouth. Though he knew it was wrong, never had the idea of kissing a woman intrigued him this way. And clearly whatever craziness was causing this, it was doing the same to her. He could tell, by the sudden shift in her demeanor, by the look in her eyes, that she was going to kiss him again. And he wasn't entirely sure he wanted to stop her.

Not only did he not stop her, but as she rose up, he leaned in to meet her halfway.

Their lips touched and whatever was left of his common sense evaporated with their mingling breath. His only coherent thought was *more*. Whatever she was willing to give, he would take.

So thank God Celia chose that exact instant to call up from the base of the stairs, "The tea is ready!"

Katy pulled away from him, eyes wide with the realization of what they had just done.

"We'll be down in a minute," he called to Celia.

"Oh, my God," she whispered, reaching up to touch her lips. "Did you *feel* that?"

Feel it? His heart was about to pound out of his chest. And he couldn't stop looking at her mouth.

He needed to get a hold of himself.

"Okay, this is not that bad," she said, trying to rationalize a situation that was completely *ir-*

rational. "We're both disappointed, and upset. That's all. This doesn't mean anything. Right?"

Leave it to Katy to take the situation and blow it wide open.

"Right. We're just upset." He didn't know if he actually believed it, but it seemed to be what she needed to hear. Why couldn't she be one of those women who was content to pretend everything was fine. Like Becca. It had been like pulling teeth to get her to admit when there was a problem, or she was upset about something.

Of course, that had been no picnic, either. Was there no happy medium?

"We need to call the doctor's office," Katy said. "Find out what we should do."

He was glad one of them was thinking clearly. Because the only clear thought he was having right now was how much he'd like to see her naked again.

They had opened a door, and he couldn't help wondering if it was only a matter of time before someone stepped through.

She had kissed Adam. On the mouth.

One minute Katy had been racked with guilt

that the procedure hadn't worked, and the next she was practically crawling out of her skin, she was so hot for him. And thank God for Celia and her timing, or who knows what *might* have happened. The possibilities both horrified and intrigued her. Though Becca was gone, he would always be her brother-in-law. Her sister's husband. To Katy *and* her parents, who would kill her if they had any clue what had just happened.

Sure, she'd hoped she and Adam could get to know each other, but she'd never meant in the *biblical* sense. Talk about going from one extreme to another.

Like her mom had so eloquently put it, he wasn't like them. So whatever was causing these weird feelings was going to have to stop.

Despite the fact that they both seemed determined to forget it happened, their trip to the doctor's office later that afternoon had been tense. But at least the appointment with Dr. Meyer had been encouraging. He assured her that she'd done nothing to cause the implantation to fail. He wrote her a prescription for hormone shots that she would begin taking a week before the next scheduled implantation. He explained that it could make her womb more hospitable and increase their chances for success.

She wasn't sure what the shots were actually doing for her womb, but as she drove back to El Paso the morning of the second procedure, her emotions were in a hopeless tangle. What if things were completely awkward between her and Adam? He had emailed her a few times in the past week to check on her, but they hadn't actually talked since her last visit.

Like last time, she drove straight to Adam's house, then Reece took her in the limo to the clinic. She assumed Adam would already be waiting in the lobby, and she was so nervous about seeing him again her hands were trembling. But he wasn't there yet. She waited in their usual spot by the elevator, wringing her hands. He sent her a text message a few minutes later that said he was running late, and to go on up without him.

What if he didn't make it on time? Would they wait for him? The idea of doing this alone made her heart race.

She took the elevator up to the clinic. She checked in, hoping they would make her wait this time, but the nurse called her back right away. She took her time changing into a gown, her anxiety mounting, waiting for a reply saying that he'd arrived. But when the nurse took her to the procedure room, she had no choice but to leave her phone in her purse.

He wasn't going to make it, she realized. Was he really held up at work, or avoiding her? Had that kiss done more damage than she'd realized? This was starting to become a familiar cycle for her. Get close to a man, let her guard down, then inevitably drive him away. What other conclusion could she draw, but that there was something seriously wrong with her? She was like a human deflector. Men got close, then bounced off the surface.

Most of her friends were already married and starting families. And here she was having a baby for someone else, because she was so unappealing, so unlovable no one wanted her.

The nurse got her situated on the table and ready for the transfer. She must have sensed Katy was upset because she put a hand on her shoulder and asked, "You okay, honey?"

Tears welled in her eyes. "I don't think Adam is going to make it."

"Mr. Blair is already here, in the waiting room."

"He is?"

She nodded and smiled. "I was just about to go get him."

She was so relieved, if she hadn't been lying down, her knees probably would have given out.

The nurse slipped out into the hall, returning a minute later with Adam. She was so happy to see him she had to bite down hard on her lip to keep from bursting into tears, but they started leaking out of her eyes anyway.

Looking worried, Adam grabbed a chair and sat down beside her. "Katy, what's the matter? Why are you crying?"

"I thought you weren't coming," she said, her voice wobbly.

"I told you I'd just be a few minutes late."

She wiped her eyes. "I know. I don't know what's wrong with me."

"It's probably the hormones you've been taking," the nurse said, handing her a tissue. "It makes some women weepy."

In that case she hoped it worked this time, so she didn't have to take this emotional rollercoaster ride again. For someone who barely even suffered PMS, this was the pits.

"Is there anything I can do?" Adam asked, looking so adorably helpless, she could have hugged him. Or kissed him. He was sitting awfully close. If she just reached up and slipped a hand around his neck, pulled him down…

Ugh. Had she really just gone from weeping, to fantasizing about jumping him? As if things weren't weird enough already.

She really was a basket case.

The door opened and Dr. Meyer came in, asking cheerfully, "Are we ready to make a baby?"

Katy nodded and held her hand out to Adam. He took it, cradling it between his, holding tight while the doctor did the transfer. Just like the last time it was quick, and mostly painless.

"You know the drill," the nurse told them when it was over. "Two hours on your back."

The nurse stepped out into the hall and it was just the two of them. Alone. Last time Adam had let go of her hand as soon as the procedure was finished, but not now. Maybe he didn't think she was so terrible after all.

"I'm really sorry about earlier," she said. "I

never cry. Not even when I was thrown from a horse and busted my collarbone. But it seems as though every time I see you now I'm blubbering about something."

"Katy, I understand."

"I just don't want you to think I'm a big baby." Because that's sure what she felt like.

"I don't. The same thing happened to Becca when they were getting her ready to harvest the eggs. Then they found the cancer and, well, suffice it to say that didn't help matters."

It was hard to imagine Becca crying about anything. Even the cancer. She had always been so strong, so determined to beat it. Even near the end, when all hope was lost, she was tough. Around Katy and their parents anyway.

"Sometimes I feel guilty that I don't miss her more," she said. "That we drifted so far apart."

"It happens, I guess."

"It's really sad. She was my sister for twenty-four years, but I don't think she ever really knew me."

That seemed to surprise him. "In what way?"

"She always thought that by staying on the ranch with our parents, I was settling—giving in—or something. She must have told me a million times that I was wasting my education. And my life. She said I should move to the city, try new things. Meet new people. And no matter how many times I told her that I loved working on the ranch, that it was what made me happy, she just didn't seem to get it. If it wasn't good enough for her, then it wasn't good enough for anyone. It was so...*infuriating.*"

"What she thought shouldn't have mattered."

But it did. She had always looked up to Becca. She was beautiful and popular and sophisticated. Of course, she could also be self-centered and stubborn, too.

"I felt as though she never really saw me. The *real* me. To her I was always little Katy, young and naive. I think she expected me to be just like her. And not only did I not give a damn about being rich and sophisticated, I could never pine for a man the way she did for you. It's like she was obsessed. Everything she did was to keep you happy. To keep you interested. It just seemed...exhausting."

Adam frowned, and Katy felt a stab of guilt.

What had possessed her to say something so insensitive?

"Oh, shoot. Adam, I'm sorry." She squeezed his hand, wishing she could take the words back. "I didn't mean to imply—"

"No, you're right. She was like that. But for the life of me I could never understand why. She didn't need to work to keep me interested. I loved her unconditionally. She was so independent and feisty."

Katy smiled. "She was definitely feisty. Full of piss and vinegar, my grandma used to say."

"She lost that. I don't know why, but after we got married, she changed."

"Maybe she loved you so much, she was afraid of losing you. Maybe she was worried that once you were married, you would get bored with her."

"That's ridiculous."

"When she met you, she seemed truly happy for the first time in her life. She was never happy at home. She never came out and said it, but we knew she was ashamed of where she came from. You'll never know how much that hurt my parents."

He surprised her by turning his hand and

threading his fingers through hers. "I tried to get Becca to visit more. I told her I would make time. I had no family, so I knew how important it was. She just…" He shrugged helplessly.

That should have hurt, but mostly Katy just felt disappointed. Especially since Becca had led them to believe that it was Adam who never had time for them.

"It was like that with the fertility treatments, too," he said. "They found the cancer, and wanted to do the surgery and start treatment immediately. She flat-out refused. She wanted to harvest her eggs. I begged her to reconsider, but she knew it was our last chance to have a child that was biologically ours. There was no reasoning with her. The doctors warned her that she had a particularly aggressive strain, but she wouldn't budge."

Becca had always led Katy and her parents to believe that Adam had been the one to make that decision, that he insisted they wait and harvest the eggs first, and they had believed her. Had it all been a lie, to shelter herself from her parents' disapproval?

Why did she portray him to be so unreasonable and demanding?

"You want to hear the really ironic part of all this?" Adam said. "I don't think she really even wanted kids."

It was true Becca had never been much of a kid person. Katy had been a little surprised when she mentioned they were trying to get pregnant. But when it didn't happen right away she'd been devastated. Because when Becca wanted something, she didn't like to wait. After that, it was as if she was obsessed. "For a year that's all she talked about," she told Adam.

"Because she knew it was what *I* wanted."

"Why wouldn't she want kids?"

"I think…I think she was afraid that if we had a child, I might love it more than her. She wanted to be the center of my universe, and I think she believed that the baby would replace her."

Was she really that insecure? She was smart and beautiful and talented with a husband who loved her. Why couldn't she just be happy? Why did she have to make everything so complicated?

"I loved Becca," Adam said, "but I don't think I ever completely understood her. But that wasn't her fault. I should have tried harder, made more of an effort. I'll regret that for the rest of my life."

It occurred to her suddenly that she and Adam were talking. Having an honest conversation. And she hadn't even been trying. It just…happened.

She and Adam were from totally different worlds. So why, at that very moment, did he feel like an equal? Not a billionaire oil man, but just a man.

Nine

Something was off.

Katy jolted awake and opened her eyes, expecting to be in her bed at home, but as her eyes adjusted she realized she was in the spare room at Adam's house.

For a second she was confused, then she remembered they'd had the embryos implanted that morning.

She must have fallen asleep during the movie they were watching. She would check the time on the digital clock on the dresser, but that would necessitate her rolling over, and she was too comfortable to move. She must have conked out a while ago because the television had gone into sleep mode. She wondered why Adam hadn't switched it off when he left.

She usually slept pretty light, so she was surprised she hadn't felt him get out of bed. He'd sat there beside her almost the entire time they had been back from Dr. Meyer's office. She hadn't even cared that he'd spent part of the time working on his laptop. She was content to just sit beside him reading the novel she'd brought with her. She even told him it was okay if he would be more comfortable working in his office. His reply was that they were in this together, and if she had to lie around all day, it was only fair he did the same. He was turning out to be a lot nicer than she ever expected. Still a bit dark and mysterious, but at least he'd opened up to her a little today.

She thought about her mother's warning, how Katy always fell hard and fast. Maybe she did have the slightest bit of a crush on Adam, but she knew better than to think it would amount to anything. She was finished with one-way relationships. And men like Adam didn't get serious about women like her. They had absolutely *nothing* in common.

Was she attracted to him? Of course. When they kissed had she practically burst into flames? She sure had, but all that meant was that they were attracted to each other.

And was she tempted by the thought of taking that attraction out for a quick spin? *Hell, yes!* But she knew that would only lead to getting her heart crushed, and who needed that? The trick was to keep herself out of temptation's way.

And what was the point of lying here in the dark obsessing about it when what she needed was a good night's sleep?

She closed her eyes, willing herself to relax. She was just starting to drift back off when she felt the bed move. If she were at home she would just assume Sylvester had jumped into bed with her. But as far as she knew Adam didn't have a cat.

Maybe it had been her imagination.

Curious, she reached back, patting the covers behind her, her hand landing on something warm and solid. She yanked it back and looked over her shoulder. The reason she hadn't felt Adam get out of bed was because he never had!

Oh, good Lord.

Was it a coincidence that she'd just been thinking about avoiding temptation, and here it was, lying right beside her? Maybe it was fate. Or a sign.

It was a sign, all right. A sign that she needed to wake him up and get him the hell out of here.

She rolled over. He was lying on his side facing her, one arm under his head. She reached out to shake him awake, then stopped just shy of touching his arm. He was so serious all the time. Even when he smiled there was an undercurrent of tension, as if he was always plotting, always planning his next move. Now he looked so…peaceful.

As if it possessed a will of its own, her hand moved to his face instead, but until she felt the rasp of his beard stubble against her fingers, she didn't think she would be bold enough to actually touch him. And now that she had, she couldn't seem to make herself stop.

There was a small white scar just below his lip where the skin was smooth and she couldn't resist tracing it with her finger. The mouth that sometimes appeared so hard and unrelenting looked soft and tender while he slept. She wanted to touch that, too. With her fingers. And her lips.

The idea of actually doing it, touching her lips to his again, made her scalp tingle.

This is a bad idea, she told herself, but knowing that didn't stop her. In fact, it made doing it even more exciting. Because honestly, when did she ever do anything that was bad for her? As long as she could remember, she'd been the good girl. The obedient daughter. Didn't she deserve to take something for herself? Just this once?

Heart pounding, she leaned close, touching her lips to his chin. He didn't wake up, didn't even stir, so she moved up a little, to the corner of his mouth, and pressed her lips there, quickly, then pulled back to check his face. His eyes were still closed. The man slept like the dead.

Trembling with anticipation, she closed her eyes and very gently pressed her lips to his... and almost moaned it felt so nice. And there it was again, that curious feeling, just like before. *Awareness.* Like a magnet pull, drawing her closer to him. She wanted to curl herself around his body, sink into his warmth. She would crawl inside his skin if she could.

She realized her lips were still pressed to his, and without meaning to, she'd gotten a little bit carried away. She opened her eyes, to make sure he was still asleep, but Adam's eyes were open, too, and he was looking right at her.

She sucked in a surprised breath, and backed away, sure that she must have looked like a deer in headlights.

She waited for him to berate her, to ask her what the hell she thought she was doing. Instead he blinked several times, eyes foggy from sleep and asked in gravelly voice, "Did you just kiss me?"

Okay, so maybe he wasn't as awake as he looked. Maybe she could lie and say it had been an accident. She had just leaned too close and accidentally bumped lips with him. He would buy that, right?

He was asleep, not stupid.

"Katy?" he said, waiting for an answer.

"Yes," she choked out, shame burning her cheeks. Not only for what she'd done, but for the fact that she wanted to do it again. "I'm sorry. I don't know what I was thinking."

She braced herself for the anger, but instead Adam touched her face…so tenderly that shivers of pleasure danced along her spine. Then he looked her right in the eye and said in a voice thick with desire, "Do it again."

He *wanted* her to kiss him?

Katy was too dumbfounded to move, but Adam apparently didn't want to wait, because he leaned in and kissed her first.

She discovered the instant their lips touched that it was a heck of a lot more fun kissing him when he was actually participating. It was exciting and terrifying and confusing and…wonderful. And it was obvious, after several minutes of making out like sex-starved teenagers, when he rolled her over onto her back and tugged her pajama top up over her head, this was going way beyond kissing. She may have started this, but it was clear that Adam intended to finish it.

What are you doing? the rational part of her brain demanded, that part that wasn't drowning in estrogen and pheromones. *This is* Adam, *your* brother-in-law. *Your* sister's *husband. This is wrong.*

But it was hard to take her rational self seriously when Adam was kissing her senseless and sliding his hand inside her pajama bottoms. She moaned as his fingers found the place where she was already hot and wet.

Already? Who was she kidding? Since she started the hormone shots she'd been walking around in a near-constant state of sexual arousal. It wasn't unusual for her to feel heightened sexual awareness when she was ovulating, but this was horny times fifty.

Maybe this had been inevitable. And maybe it made her a lousy sister, or just a terrible person in general, but she didn't care. She wanted him. She had never done a truly selfish thing in her life, but she was going to do this.

And she would *not* fall in love with him.

She fumbled with the buttons on Adam's shirt, her fingers clumsy and uncooperative, until she got fed up and just ripped the damned thing open. If he cared that she'd just ruined his shirt he didn't say so. Of course, he was a little preoccupied driving her crazy with his fingers and his mouth.

She shoved the shirt off his shoulders and down his arms, her eyes raking over his chest. Swirls of black hair circled small dark nipples then narrowed into a trail down the center of his lean stomach, disappearing under the waistband of his slacks.

Breathless with excitement, she put her hands on him. His skin was hot and she could feel the heavy thump of his heart. She wanted to touch him everywhere.

She half expected him to be as controlled and closed off as he always was. Hadn't Becca confided to her that sex with Adam was "nice," but sometimes she wished he would be a little more passionate, more adventurous? But Adam must have changed, because if he were any more passionate than he was now, they would set the sheets on fire. He was reckless and impulsive and…crazy.

They kissed and touched, tore at each other's clothes. There was barely a second when his mouth wasn't somewhere on her body. Her lips, her breasts, the column of her throat. He licked and nibbled as if he wanted to eat her alive. Until the sensations all started to run together, and her entire being quivered with the need for release.

And when she didn't think she could stand much more, when she felt she would go out of her mind if he didn't *take* her, he said, "I have to make love to you."

Not he *wanted* to, but he *had* to. As in, he wanted it so badly, he couldn't stop himself. And she felt exactly the same way.

As he centered himself between her thighs, his strong arms caging her, she considered fleetingly that maybe they shouldn't be doing this, but as he thrust inside her, her brain could do nothing but feel. Feel his hands and his mouth. Feel the slow, steady rhythm of his body moving inside of hers, connecting in a way she had never imagined. It felt as if she had been working up to this moment her entire life. Every man who had come before him…they hadn't come close to making her feel what she did now. Excited and humbled and terrified all at once. And as she cried out with release, felt Adam shudder and then go still inside of her, she was terrified that no one ever would again.

Because as earth-shatteringly wonderful as this

had been, this was Adam, her brother-in-law. He was a billionaire oil man and she was a rancher. He wore thousand-dollar suits to work and she spent her days wading through cow manure.

They were worse than oil and water. They were gasoline and a lit match. And she could tell, by the way he rolled over and lay silently beside her, the only sound his breath coming in sharp rasps, he was probably thinking the same thing. He was probably afraid that she had just fallen head over heels in love with him, and was wondering how he was going to let her down easy.

Well, he didn't have to worry about her. She was firmly rooted in reality.

She took a deep breath, blew it out and said, "Despite what you're probably thinking right now, this was not a big deal."

Not a big deal?
Adam lay beside Katy, trying to catch his breath, after what was by far the best sex of his entire adult life.

Despite the fact that it was over *way* too fast. But it had been almost four years since he'd been with a woman, so the fact that he'd lasted more than thirty seconds was, in his opinion, a small miracle.

Then he had a thought, one that just about stopped his pulse. "Were we supposed to do that?"

"Well, given the nature of our relationship—"

"No, I mean, was that on the list?"

"List?"

"The things you're not supposed to do after the embryo transfer."

He heard her inhale sharply, then she jolted up in bed. "I don't know."

"I don't recall the doctor mentioning anything about sex, but I could swear there was something on the list." He might have thought of it sooner, but when he woke to discover her kissing him, his brain must have shorted out.

"Do you still have the list?" she asked. "I think I left it here the last time."

"I think Celia put it on my desk."

She swung her legs over the side of the bed and he grabbed her arm. "You're on bed rest. I'll go."

She looked at him like he was an idiot, since she was probably thinking that the damage had already been done. But technically she was still on bed rest, and since she hadn't actually gotten out of bed, maybe they were okay. He switched on the lamp, blinking against the sudden bright light. He found his pants on the floor beside the bed and yanked them on. Then he turned and saw Katy sitting there naked, fishing her panties from between the covers, her skin rosy, her breasts covered with love bites, and almost took them back off again.

He actually paused for a second and reached for his fly, then thought, *What the hell are you doing?* They shouldn't have slept together the first time, but once could at least be written off as sexual curiosity. Or temporary insanity. The second time, though, showed intent. It implied a relationship, and he sure as hell didn't want that.

He didn't care how fantastic the sex was. There was no way it was going to happen again.

He left Katy wrestling with her undergarments and headed down to his office. He found the list buried under a month's worth of miscellaneous papers. He switched out the lights and took the stairs two at a time up to the bedroom.

Katy was sitting in bed, wearing her pajama top and panties, looking anxious.

"Got it," he said, sitting beside her.

"What does it say?" she asked, leaning close to read it with him.

He saw it right away, at the bottom. He pointed to the line. "No intercourse or orgasms."

She closed her eyes and cursed. "So what does this mean?"

"That it might not work, I guess."

"And if it did work, could what we did have hurt the baby?"

"I don't know. I wouldn't think so. We'll just have to wait and ask, I guess. I wonder, though, maybe intercourse alone isn't that bad, maybe if you didn't..." He looked at her hopefully.

She looked confused, then she realized what he was implying. "Of course I did! You couldn't *tell?*"

He shrugged. She wouldn't be the first woman to...embellish. "I thought it couldn't hurt to ask."

"I'm so sorry," she said miserably, drawing her knees up to her chest and hugging them. "This is all my fault."

"No, it isn't."

"I started this. If I hadn't kissed you..."

Why did you? he wanted to ask her, but he had

the feeling he'd rather not know. Besides, it didn't even matter. It happened. The damage was done. "I could have stopped you, but I didn't."

She buried her face in her hands. "How could I let this happen?"

"It's been an emotional couple of weeks for both of us. We made a mistake."

"We definitely can't do this again," she said.

"I agree."

"I mean, it was great, but…well…you know."

He was a little curious to know what she meant. What he was supposed to know. If for no other reason than to see if they had the same reasons, but at this point it didn't seem to matter.

They sat there in awkward silence for a minute or two. What was left to say at this point? "I should leave you alone, so you can get some rest."

She fidgeted with the edge of the blanket. "I do have a long drive tomorrow."

He got up and grabbed his shredded shirt from where it had landed on the floor. "Try not to worry. If it doesn't work, we'll try again."

"And we're never doing *this* again," she said, gesturing to the bed, as if he wasn't already clear on that point.

"Like you said, it's not a big deal. It doesn't change anything. It happened, and it won't happen again."

He couldn't tell if she looked relieved or disappointed, and the truth was, he really didn't want to know.

Ten

The next ten days were the longest in Katy's life. She tried to keep herself busy with work, but even putting together the ranch's quarterly taxes wasn't enough to distract her from the guilt that she might have completely blown their chances to conceive. And she didn't care what Adam said. It was her fault. He never would have made the first move.

Though she tried to put on a good face for her parents, they could tell she was upset. She told them she was just worried that it wouldn't work, but she didn't tell them why. How could she?

By the way, Mom and Dad, did I mention that I

seduced and slept with my dead sister's husband? They would never forgive her. And she couldn't blame them. She wasn't even sure if she could forgive herself.

She did try to talk to her mom about Adam, and how he wasn't the man they thought he was, and her mom got that, "Oh, no, here we go again, Katy has a crush" look, so she didn't even bother. Maybe because she was too ashamed to admit that her mom had been right. Although it was obvious by how readily Adam agreed it was a mistake, that he hadn't spontaneously fallen madly in love with her.

She wished she could say the same. But that was her own fault. Still, he was all she could think about lately. She probably wouldn't have minded him inundating her with calls and emails this time, but he seemed to know instinctively that it was better to back off. He'd text messaged her a couple of times, to see how she was feeling.

She kept waiting for some sort of sign, to start *feeling* pregnant.

"I knew right away," her best friend Missy told her as she fixed a bottle for the three-month-old strapped to her chest, while balancing a toddler on one hip and dodging the groping hands of the three- and five-year-olds. "My mood changed and my hair started falling out. Not like I was going bald," she added at Katy's look of horror. "But it got thinner during all my pregnancies."

"I don't feel anything," Katy told her.

"Oh, sweetie," she had said clucking sympathetically. "I'm sure it will work. And if it doesn't, you'll just try again. The doctors can only do so much. You have to trust your body to do the rest."

But she had betrayed her body. She didn't give it a chance to do the rest. And talking to Missy only made her feel worse because she was even more convinced that she wasn't pregnant. Because she didn't feel *any* different than before. Other than the crushing guilt that she had set Adam's baby plan back at least a month, not to mention that he only had two more viable embryos. Then the only thing left of her sister would be gone forever.

How would she live with herself if she had ruined this for him?

This had been so much easier when she didn't like him. When she thought he was a cold, arrogant jerk.

The morning of their next appointment, Katy drove to El Paso feeling like she had a boulder in her chest, convinced the transfer didn't take. If it had, she would have felt something by now. Some subtle sign that her body was changing. But there was nothing. Not a twinge or a flutter, no weird food cravings or morning sickness. She was so sure her period would start she almost hadn't bothered to come, but it would be her only chance to see Adam for at least another few weeks, when they did the final transfer.

And if that didn't work? Well, there was a good chance she might never see him again. And who knows, maybe it would be for the best.

She had herself so worked into a lather that when she stepped through the doors to the lobby of the medical building and saw Adam standing by the elevators waiting for her, she immediately burst into tears. Mortified beyond belief, she turned right back around and walked out.

She heard the door open behind her, and hurried footsteps in her direction, then she felt his hand on her shoulder. "Katy, what's wrong?"

She shook her head, unable to speak.

His arms went around her, pulling her against

his chest. And even though she knew she was only torturing herself, she sank into him. Clung to him. Why did she do this to herself? Why did she fall for men who didn't want her?

He stroked her hair, her back. "Talk to me, Katy. What's wrong?"

Only *everything.*

"I'm not pregnant," she said miserably, burying her face against his chest.

"You started your period?"

"No, but…I just know. It didn't work."

"You don't know that," he said patiently.

"I do, and it's all my fault."

"Listen to me. You have to stop blaming yourself. And what's the point in getting so upset if you don't even know for sure?"

"I told you, I just know. I don't *feel* pregnant."

"That doesn't mean you aren't." He took her by the shoulders and held her at arm's length. "Calm down, and let's go inside and get the test. Then we'll know definitively if you are or aren't."

"And if I'm not?"

"Let's worry about that when the time comes, okay?"

She nodded and wiped her cheeks.

With a hand on her back, as if he thought she might try to make a run for it, Adam led her back through the door and up to the clinic.

They had to sit in the general waiting room this time, with half a dozen other couples, several of whom were clearly expecting. Happy couples who loved each other. Which of course only made her feel worse.

When the nurse finally called them back Katy was on the verge of tears again. Adam must have realized because he took her hand and gave it a reassuring squeeze. The nurse drew blood, slapped a bandage on, and said, "I'll send this right to the lab and we'll call later this afternoon with the results."

"How much later?" Adam asked.

"Usually between three and four. Sometimes earlier. It just depends how busy they are."

"That's it?" Katy asked. "We don't see the doctor?"

"Not until after you get your results."

They stopped at the front desk on their way out, and Adam was able to get them an appointment for seven that evening, so she wouldn't have to make the long drive out again.

"I'm not letting you drive home that late," Adam said when they met back at his house and she mentioned leaving straight from Dr. Meyer's office. He opened the front door, disengaged the alarm, and gestured her inside. "You can stay with me."

"I'm not sure if that's a good idea."

"You don't trust me?"

She didn't trust herself. Especially not when he'd been so touchy-feely with her. Hugging her and holding her hand. It was torture. What would he do if she made the first move again? Would he give in and make love to her? Or would he push her away this time?

She wouldn't be finding out, because the possibility that he would reject her would be more than she could bear.

She followed him into the kitchen. "It's not that I don't trust you," she said. "It'll just be...awkward."

He stopped and turned to her. "Katy, if we're going to make this surrogacy thing work, we have to get past what happened. If you can't do that—"

"Of course I can." It was obviously just a little

harder for her than it was for him. "You're right. I'll stay here."

He pulled two bottles of water out of the fridge and handed her one. "So, what would you like to do until the doctor's office calls?"

"Don't you have to go back to work?"

He leaned against the edge of the counter. "Nope. I'm yours all day."

Oh, didn't she wish.

"We could go for a swim," he said.

"I didn't bring a suit." Or pajamas, or clothes for the next day, she realized.

He shrugged. "Who needs bathing suits? It's not like I haven't seen it before. Right?"

Her heart slammed the wall of her chest. She was too stunned to reply. Hope welled up inside of her, then fizzled out when she saw the corner of his mouth tip up and realized that he was kidding.

"That was a joke," she said.

"Yeah. It was a joke."

Not only did he have a sense of humor, but it was warped. And he obviously had no idea what he'd just done to her. Why would he? She was the one who'd said it meant nothing. Right? He had no idea how conflicted she felt. And she intended to keep it that way.

"Celia has a whole cabinet full of bathing suits in the cabana. There's bound to be one that will fit you."

Since they didn't have anything better to do, and they could take their cell phones with them by the pool, why not? But of course she found out *why not* when she walked out of the cabana, in the modest one-piece she'd found in her size, to find Adam standing by the pool, bare-chested, his bronze skin glistening in the sun, making him look like a Greek Adonis. He looked *really* good for forty. In fact, he could totally put to shame most of the twenty-something guys she knew. His body was truly a work of art. And she was stuck looking at it for God only knows how long.

Hey, it could be worse, she thought. He could be wearing a Speedo.

Since she didn't want to be away from her phone, she only waded around for a few minutes, then she laid back in one of the lounge chairs, sipping iced tea and watching Adam do laps. She recalled Becca telling her once that he'd been on the swim team in college. He'd been so good that later he had a shot at making the Olympic team, but had to drop out when his father died so he could take over Western Oil. She would have to ask him about that some time.

Or not. Probably the less she got to know him, the better. Why make it harder on herself?

Around one Celia brought out a tray of cheese enchiladas and homemade tamales, and though Katy was hungry, and the food was delicious, she was too nervous to eat much. She kept looking at the cell phones sitting side by side on the table, willing them to ring. And at the same time she was dreading it.

An hour later Celia left to do some shopping, and at three Katy and Adam had had enough sun and decided to go in. She was in the kitchen refilling her iced tea, and he was about to go take a quick shower, when his cell phone started to rumble on the counter. Then it started to ring.

For a second they both just stood there looking at it, as though it were some deadly venomous insect neither wanted to touch. Then Adam sighed, grabbed it off the counter and answered.

"Yes, this is he," he said to the caller, and though she could hear someone talking, she couldn't hear what they were saying. She stood there with her heart in her throat, waiting. He said, "uh-huh" twice and "we'll be there," then he hung up.

She was gripping the edge of the counter, hands trembling, and her heart was thumping out about a thousand beats per minute. "Well, what did they say?"

Adam shook his head, looking shell-shocked, and her heart plummeted. She was right. It hadn't work. They blew it. Then he said, "Positive."

It took a second to process, then she repeated, to be sure she hadn't heard him wrong, *"Positive?"*

He nodded.

"This isn't a joke? It's really positive? It worked?"

A grin spread across his face. "It worked. You're pregnant."

All the stress and grief, and every other emotion that had been building for the last ten days welled up like a geyser and erupted in a whoop of joy that her parents probably heard all the way in Peckins.

In one minute she was across the room, and the

next she was in Adam's arms and he was hugging her tight.

"I guess you're happy," he said, and though she couldn't see it, because she was plastered against him, she could hear the smile in his voice.

More than just being happy that she was pregnant, that at least one of the embryos had attached, she was relieved that she hadn't screwed things up for him. She could stop feeling guilty. She could stop thinking back to that night and berating herself for kissing him in the first place, and for not stopping him when he kissed her back, and started undressing her.

Touching her.

Sort of like right now, she realized, as she became aware that her breasts were crushed against his bare chest, that his hands were on her bare back. He smelled like chlorine and sunblock, and his skin felt hot to the touch. And it took exactly two seconds to realize that hugging him had been a terrible mistake.

But why wasn't he letting go? And why were his hands sliding farther south, dangerously close to her behind.

"Um, Adam?"

"Yeah?"

"Maybe you should, you know…let go of me."

"I probably should," he said, nuzzling the side of her throat.

Oh, good Lord.

"Okay…*now*," she said, but he didn't let go. But to be fair, neither did she. Then she felt his lips on her neck and her legs nearly gave out.

"Katy?"

"Huh?"

"I think I have to kiss you again."

There it was again, that "have to" line.

"I really wish you wouldn't," she said, but his hands were already sliding up her back, tangling through her hair.

Oh, hell, here we go again, she thought as he eased her head back and crushed his lips down on hers. It was so hot she was sure she would melt into a puddle on the kitchen floor.

Did the man have to be such a good kisser.

"Hey Adam, are you two—oops!"

They both jumped a mile and swiftly untangled themselves from each other. Celia stood in the kitchen doorway, her arms filled with reusable canvas grocery bags.

"I'm sorry," she said, looking embarrassed. "I didn't mean to...interrupt."

Everyone seemed at a loss for words, so Katy said what she could to fill the awkward silence.

"We just heard from the doctor's office." As if that brought logic to their passionate embrace. "I'm pregnant!"

Eleven

According to the ultrasound Dr. Meyer performed at their appointment later that evening, she was pregnant with a single embryo.

After a brief examination, he showed them to his private office and explained just about everything she and Adam needed to know about her pregnancy—she was honestly, truly *pregnant!* What changes to expect in her body, and the things she should and shouldn't eat. The kind of activity that was safe and what medications weren't. And her due date, which they learned was early the following spring.

But now the appointment was almost over and

neither had mentioned the one thing they both needed to know. It was the huge pink elephant in the room. And since Adam didn't seem inclined to ask, it was up to her to put it out there.

"If you have any other questions for me—" the doctor started to say, and Katy said, "I have one."

She looked over at Adam and he had a slightly pained look on his face. "Suppose, *hypothetically*, that a surrogate were to have sex right after the transfer. Could that hurt the baby in any way?"

The doctor looked up sharply from the notes he'd been jotting in her file. "You didn't, did you?"

His reaction startled her.

It couldn't be that bad, could it? "Even if we did, the embryo latched on," she rationalized. "So no harm done. Right?"

"Successful implantation is only part of the reason. For surrogates like yourself, who have no known fertility issues, there's also the problem of conception."

"But didn't we want her to conceive?" Adam asked, before she had the chance.

"In all likelihood, because the embryos were implanted at the most fertile stage in her cycle, her body also released its own healthy and viable egg. And I'm sure I don't have to explain to either of you what happens if you introduce sperm with an egg."

Katy's stomach bottomed out, and Adam went pale.

The doctor looked from Adam to Katy. "Gauging by your reactions, should I assume this might be the case?"

"So what you're saying," Adam clarified, as if it wasn't crystal clear already, "is that it could be Katy's own fertilized egg, and not one of the embryos."

"It could be."

Katy felt sick to her stomach. This could not possibly be happening.

Under the circumstances, Adam sounded unusually calm and detached when he asked, "Is there any way to tell?"

"Only though a DNA test. Either after the birth, or through amniocentesis."

"How soon could the amnio be done?" Adam asked.

"At the earliest, fourteen weeks, but I do have to warn you that there are risks involved."

"What kind of risks?"

"Infection, miscarriage."

Katy stared at him, slack-jawed, feeling as though she had just taken the leading role in the world's most horrific waking nightmare.

"So what kind of odds are we looking at?" Adam asked. How could he be so *calm?* Panic was clawing at her insides. It was all she could do not to get up and pace the room like a caged animal.

"Of course, I can't be certain, but I would put the odds at somewhere in the ball park of five to one."

She felt a slight tug of relief. As far as odds went, that wasn't *too* bad.

"Five to one that it was one of the embryos?" Adam clarified.

"No. That it was Katy's own egg."

Oh, crap.

Katy felt light-headed, like she might faint. What the *hell* had they done? Having her sister's baby was one thing, but to have her own baby, and with Adam of all people? This was crazy!

She wasn't ready to have a child yet, especially not with her sister's husband! A man she loved, whose only interest in her was to produce his offspring.

She had a sudden and disturbing vision of her family up on the stage during a *Jerry Springer* episode.

Her family. Oh, God. How was she going to explain this to her parents? They had been so excited when she called to tell them the good news earlier. They would be furious enough if they knew she had slept with Adam, but to learn she could be having her own baby, not Becca's? They might never speak to her again.

Adam put his hand on her arm. She looked up at him and he gestured to the door. She realized, the appointment was over. There was nothing else the doctor could do for them at this point. From now on it would just be a waiting game. At least twelve more weeks.

It sounded like a lifetime.

Her legs felt unsteady as Adam led her out. She only half heard him as he stopped to make next month's appointment, then he ushered her out of the office and to the elevator. He was taking this awfully well.

"I can't believe this is happening," she said, as the elevator doors slid closed. "This is all my—"

"If you say it's your fault one more time, I swear to God I'm going to make you *walk* home," he said sharply, his eyes flashing with anger.

Whoa.

So much for him taking it well. Apparently he was as freaked out as she was. He was just better at hiding it.

He took a deep breath and blew it out. "I'm sorry. I didn't mean to snap. I just think that blaming each other, or ourselves, isn't going to get us anywhere. It's happened, and now we have to figure out the best way to deal with the situation."

She nodded.

Reece was waiting for them when they walked out of the building. After they got in the limo, Adam asked, "Would you like to stop someplace and get dinner?"

The thought of food made her stomach roil. "I'm really not hungry right now."

"You've hardly eaten a thing all day. It's not healthy to skip meals."

Nor would it be healthy to eat a meal, then barf

it back up, which is what would probably happen. "I'll have something later. I promise."

They were silent for the rest of the drive back to his place. She figured they would talk later that evening, after they'd each had a chance to process it, but as they walked inside she was hit with a wave of fatigue so intense she knew she needed to rest first. She was so exhausted she tripped on the foyer step and would have fallen on her face if Adam hadn't caught her by the arm.

"You okay," he asked, brow creased with worry.

"Just really tired. I think I need to lie down."

"You know we need to talk."

"I know. And I'm not trying to avoid it. Maybe if I sleep for an hour or so, I'll feel better."

"Of course," he said, leading her upstairs to the spare room.

"Would you possibly have an old shirt or something that I can sleep in? I didn't know I would be staying over so I didn't bring extra clothes." She felt uncomfortable enough sleeping here, where this nightmare of a situation had been conceived, she couldn't imagine doing it in her underwear.

"I'm sure I can dig up something." He left for several minutes, then reappeared with a long-sleeved, button-down silk pajama top. "Will this work?"

"That's perfect. Thanks."

"I'll be in my office if you need me." He hesitated by the door, like he wanted to say something else, then he left, closing the door behind him. A second later she heard the muffled sound of him walking down the stairs.

It took all the effort she could muster to change into the pajama top, and though it was way too big for her, it was cool and soft against her skin. And even though it was freshly laundered, it smelled like Adam. That might have excited her if she hadn't been so dead on her feet. It was as if it was all just too much to take in and her body was shutting down. She crawled into bed, under the covers, and must have been out before her head even hit the pillow.

She woke later, feeling drugged and disoriented, not sure where she was, or if it was day or night. She recalled the doctor visit and for a second thought maybe it had all been a terrible dream.

But she was at Adam's house, and it hadn't been a dream. It was very, very real. She looked over at the digital clock, blinking to clear the sleep from her eyes. It read 1:15 a.m.

One-fifteen? She shot up in bed and swung her legs over the side, instantly awake. She and Adam were supposed to talk. He was waiting for her!

Then she realized, he had probably gone to bed already, and their conversation, critical as it would be, would have to wait until morning. She was disappointed, but at the same time relieved. She needed time to think this through, to wrap her head around it, and knowing Adam, he would want to make a decision right away. He would want to begin planning their next move.

She got up and used the bathroom, then brushed her teeth with a spare brush she found in the cabinet. Since she would have to wear the same clothes tomorrow for the drive home, and there was nothing she hated more than not feeling fresh, she washed her panties in the sink and hung them on the towel bar to dry.

She was about to climb back into bed when her stomach let out a hollow rumble, and she realized that she was famished. She recalled how delicious the enchiladas were that they'd had for lunch and wondered if there were any leftovers. She should really eat something. Because as Adam had pointed out, she shouldn't be skipping meals. Cliché and silly as it sounded, she was eating for two now.

She opened the door and peeked out into the hallway. The house was quiet and dark, just as she'd suspected. She felt her way down the stairs and tiptoed through the living room to the kitchen.

"Going somewhere?"

At the unexpected voice she let out a squeal of surprise, and whipped around. Adam was sitting slumped down on the couch, holding something…a drink, she realized. He was sitting in the dark drinking. Not that she could blame him. If alcohol wasn't bad for the baby, she would be drowning in it by now.

"I woke up hungry," she said. "I was going to get something to eat."

As her eyes adjusted, she could see that he was shirtless, and wearing what looked like a pair of pajama bottoms.

Oh, my.

"I though you'd gone to bed," she said.

"Couldn't sleep."

Well, that was understandable. She wondered if he was upset, or even angry with her. It was too dark to see his individual features so she really couldn't get a read on him.

"I'm sorry I slept for so long."

"S'okay."

"I wasn't trying to avoid you."

"I know."

She took a step closer. "Are you okay?"

"What do you think?"

Fair enough. "Do you want to talk?"

"Actually, I think I'd prefer you take off your clothes."

She actually jerked backward. Was that another joke? "E-excuse me?"

"I want to see you naked."

"N-naked?"

"You said before that if I wanted to see you naked, all I have to do is ask. So I'm asking."

She may have said it, but she didn't actually *mean* it. And never in a million years did she believe he would actually ask. It had to be the alcohol talking. "You're drunk."

"So what if I am?"

"So, you're clearly not thinking straight."

"Isn't that the point of drinking?" He downed the contents of his glass and set it on the table beside him. "Besides, it's not like I haven't seen you naked before."

"Yes, but don't you think it will inevitably lead to something else?"

"Again, that's kind of the point."

Her heart started to hammer. "But we said we wouldn't."

"We said a lot of things, and look where it got us. So get naked, now."

He was only doing this because he was upset and intoxicated. He didn't really want her. Not the way she wanted him. "No. I'm upset, too, but this isn't going to solve anything."

"No, but it'll feel good, and that's enough for me right now. Don't you want to feel good?"

Maybe feeling good wasn't enough for her.

But what if it was? Maybe she could have him just one more time.

No. Bad idea.

"Adam, I'm serious. Stop. We can't do this. I don't want to do this."

"Making love to you again is all I've been able to think about," he said, and his words warmed her from the inside out. Even though she knew he was only saying them because he'd been drinking and his inhibitions were compromised. And even if he had been thinking about it, it was just sex to him. It had nothing to do with love. That's the way it was for men.

The men she knew anyway.

"We shouldn't," she said, but with a dismal lack of conviction. He was starting to wear her down.

"Come here, Katy," he said, in a low growl that set every one of her nerve endings ablaze.

He reached out to grasp her wrist. She put up only the slightest bit of resistance before she let him pull her down into his lap. She was straddling his thighs, his silk pajama pants feeling unbelievably erotic on her bare bottom. Then he kissed her, tangling his fingers through her hair. Tenderly, his lips soft, his mouth sweet and tangy as his tongue slid against hers.

Wait a minute…*sweet?*

She broke the kiss and pulled back to look at him. Where was the alcohol taste? She grabbed the glass he'd been drinking out of and sniffed it. "What was this?"

"Orange juice."

"With vodka?"

"Nope. Just plain old orange juice."

"But...you said you were drunk."

"No, *you* said I was drunk. I just didn't correct you."

"But I thought—"

He didn't let her finish. He covered her lips with his and kissed away whatever she'd been about to say. He stroked and caressed away her doubts, until there was nothing left but raw need. When he pulled the pajama top up over her head and saw that she wasn't wearing panties, he growled low in his throat. "I think you forgot something."

"I didn't have a clean pair for tomorrow, so I washed them out in the sink."

"Lucky me," he murmured as he dipped his head to take her nipple in his mouth. Her entire being shuddered with ecstasy.

Adam lifted her off his lap and laid her down on the cushions, settling beside her, then he was kissing her again. Her lips and her throat, her breasts. He tortured her with nips and love bites, until she was burning up with need. He worked his way downward, across her stomach, then lower still.

She was no stranger to oral sex, although she wasn't usually the one on the receiving end. And on the rare occasion she'd been in the hot seat, the truth is it hadn't really been that fantastic. More clumsy and awkward than arousing. But as Adam slipped down onto the floor beside her, spreading her thighs to make room for himself, as his tongue lashed out to taste her, she was so close to unraveling she couldn't see straight.

Then a light switched on in the kitchen, dimly illuminating the room. She and Adam froze as they heard Celia shuffle out of her room. The couch was facing away from the light, so the only way she would know they were there was if she walked into the living room, which wasn't entirely impossible.

She heard Celia get a glass out of the cupboard, and fill it with water. She was frantically trying to recall where Adam had thrown the pajama top when she felt his tongue on her again. She was so surprised she gasped, slapping a hand over her mouth to smother the sound. What the heck was he doing? Did he *want* to get caught?

Getting caught kissing was one thing, but this? This would be absolutely mortifying.

She tried to push his head away, to close her legs, but that only seemed to fuel his determination. He pressed her thighs open even wider, devouring her. Could this possibly be the man her sister claimed wasn't *adventurous* enough? And maybe it was the element of danger, or the sheer stupidity of what they were doing, but the more she tried to fight it, the more turned on she was getting. Then Adam entered her with his fingers, thrusting them deep inside of her, and her control shattered. She buried her face in the cushion to muffle the moan of pleasure she couldn't suppress.

She'd barely had a chance to catch her breath when the light suddenly went out, and Celia shuffled back to her room behind the kitchen.

The second Katy heard the door close she gave Adam a good hard whack on the top of his head.

"Ow! What was that for?" he said, ducking away from a possible repeat attack.

"Are you crazy?" she hissed, sitting up. "She could have walked in here and seen us."

He was grinning. "But she didn't. And you can't deny that the idea of being caught was arousing as hell."

No, she couldn't deny it. But it wasn't a chance she was willing to take again. "Maybe we should move this party upstairs."

"That's probably not a bad idea."

No, it was. This whole thing was a horrible, horrible mistake. But it was too late now. He'd pleased her, and it was only fair to reciprocate. Right?

And if they were going to do this, they might as well have fun. And worry about the consequences in the morning.

She located the pajama top on the floor and pulled it on, just in case, then turned to Adam, grinning wickedly, and said, "Last one there is a rotten egg."

Twelve

Katy darted up the stairs, and Adam took off after her, catching up just outside the bedroom where she'd been sleeping. He hooked his arms around her waist, trapping her against him, and tugged in the direction of his bedroom. She pulled away from him, looking hesitant.

Confused, he asked, "What's the matter?"

"Where are we going?"

"My bedroom."

"Not there."

Because it wasn't just his bedroom, he realized. It was Becca's.

He didn't try to explain that while it was

Becca's room, too, the bed itself had to be replaced due to her illness. And that even before that, he and Becca hadn't exactly shared a lot of passionate nights there.

But he didn't want to make Katy uncomfortable, so when she took his hand and led him into the spare room, he let her.

She pulled the pajama top off and walked backward toward the bed, summoning him with a crooked finger. And when he got there she shoved him backward onto the mattress. The sheets were cool against his skin and smelled like her. He tried to pull her down beside him, but she straddled his legs instead. Her skin was flush with arousal, her nipples puckered tight. Her hair hung down in mussed curls that grazed the tops of her breasts. He'd never seen anything so sexy in his life.

She ran her hands down his chest, raking his skin with her nails. "I want to see you naked."

"All you had to do was ask," he said with a grin, and she tugged his pajama bottoms down and off his legs. Then she just stared at his erection in awe, as though she'd never seen one before.

She must have noticed his curious expression,

because she said, "I didn't get a good look the other night." She reached out and wrapped her hand around him, slowly stroking from base to tip, then back down again. "I've never seen one this big. Not that I've seen a lot of them. Only three, besides yours."

That surprised him. Not that he thought Katy was the kind to sleep around, but she had a way about her that was blatantly sexual. Like the way she was casually running her thumb over the head of his erection, making it really tough to concentrate on the conversation. "That's not many," he said.

"You know, I didn't lose my virginity until I was nineteen."

Another surprise. "Really?"

"I had done a lot of fooling around before then, but I planned to wait until I was married to actually seal the deal."

She gave him a gentle squeeze and his breath caught. "So why didn't you?"

"Because it occurred to me around then that it could take a long time to find Mr. Right, and I figured if fooling around felt good, actual sex would feel even better."

"Did it?"

She shrugged. "Not at first. But then sometimes it did, depending on who I was with. But that never really mattered because I'm completely capable of taking care of my own needs if necessary."

He didn't know who these men were she was sleeping with, but it would be a cold day in hell when he let a woman he was with "take care of her own needs."

"Is it weird that I'm telling you this?" she asked.

"Oddly enough, no." Even though he was having an increasingly difficult time concentrating on what she was saying. His gaze was fixed on her hand, sliding slowly up and down his shaft.

"When did you lose your virginity?" she asked.

"I was sixteen."

"Seriously?"

"She was eighteen."

"Ah, an older woman. Did it last?"

"About fifteen seconds."

She laughed. "I meant the relationship."

"That *was* the relationship." And he wouldn't last much longer than that now if she kept stroking him that way. "We hooked up at a party. I never saw her again."

"I've never had a one-night stand. Unless you count ten days ago." Letting go of his erection, she ran her hands up his stomach, over his chest. "But I guess after tonight we'll have to relabel it. Is there such a thing as a two-night stand?"

He didn't see any reason to slap a label on it. It was what it was.

She gazed down at him, lids heavy, cheeks rosy. "I like talking to you. And I like that you're willing to open up to me. I know that's not easy for you."

Not only did she like it, he realized that talking like this was turning her on. Like verbal foreplay.

A woman who got off on conversation. Who would have imagined? But he needed more. Less talk and more action. He needed to get his hands on her body, to be inside of her. It was all he'd been able to think about since that first time ten days ago. Looking back on it now, he should have realized that this was inevitable. That once was never going to be enough. "Why don't you make love to me," he said.

Her honey-dipped smile said she thought that

was a pretty good idea. "Like this? With me on top?"

"However you'd like." On top, on the bottom. Upside down or sideways, he didn't really care.

She rose up onto her knees, flush with anticipation and centered herself over him, then she sank down, taking him inside of her, inch by excruciating inch, until he was as far as he could go. She was hot and wet and tight.

She looked down at him, and smiled. "Hmm, that's nice."

She took the words right out of his mouth. She started to move, riding him slowly, as though she had all the time in the world. Her eyes drifted closed, head rolled back. She looked completely lost in the sensation, and he was so fascinated watching her, his own pleasure seemed almost insignificant. He was content to let her use him as long as she wanted, stroking everything he could reach. Her thighs, her stomach, her breasts. Every part of her soft and feminine.

She took one of his hands and guided it between her legs, where their bodies were joined. He rubbed her there, and she started whimpering, making soft breathy sounds. She began to tremble all over and he knew she was almost there. Then her body clamped down hard around him, clenching and releasing. Watching her come was the most erotic thing he'd ever seen, and just like that he lost it. It was sexual release like he'd never felt before, hot pulsations that robbed him of the ability to do anything but feel.

Katy crumpled into a heap on his chest, curling herself around him. He could feel her heart hammering just as hard as his own. As much as he hated to admit it, sex with Becca had never been like this. She had always been too uptight, too worried that she would disappoint him to just let loose and have fun. And when they were trying to get pregnant, sex became a job. Then she was diagnosed and that put an end to their sex life altogether.

Maybe he should have felt bad comparing the two, and guilty knowing that, as much as he loved Becca, Katy was everything he'd always hoped his wife would be in the bedroom. But he didn't. Everything else was so screwed up, this seemed to be the only thing that made any sense. Even though it made no sense at all.

Maybe this was wrong, and he would regret it

someday. All he knew was that for the past three years since Becca died he'd barely been able to look at another woman. Not a day passed that he didn't ache from missing his wife. But when he was with Katy he could forget for a while. He finally felt…at peace.

It was too bad that it had to end.

Katy woke the next morning and reached for Adam, but he wasn't there. She sat up and looked at the clock, surprised that it was almost nine-thirty. She was usually up at the crack of dawn. Of course, it had almost been the crack of dawn when Adam finally let her go to sleep.

The man had an insatiable sexual appetite, not to mention the stamina of someone half his age. After the third time she even started to wonder if he'd swallowed a couple of Viagra. Until he mentioned that, before their first night together, it had been *four* years, and suddenly it made sense. She didn't even know men could go that long without sex. She had just assumed he'd been with women since Becca died. But he was sure making up for lost time.

Now it was that dreaded morning after, and as

exciting and, for lack of a better word, *magical,* as it had been, they had to face reality. Not to mention the situation with the baby.

She rolled out of bed and took stock of the room. Blankets askew, sheet pulled off the mattress in one corner. Celia was going to walk in and know instantly that they'd had wild sex all night. Of course, they hadn't exactly been quiet, so it was possible she'd figured it out for herself already.

Just in case, Katy spent a few minutes straightening things up, then took a long, hot shower. She half hoped that Adam had gone to work, even though she knew delaying the conversation they needed to have wouldn't make it any easier. But he was sitting at the kitchen table drinking coffee and reading the *Wall Street Journal.* She'd expected him to be dressed for work, but he was wearing chinos and a polo shirt with the Western Oil logo on it. His hair was damp, so he must have gotten up not long before she did. It was the first time she had seen him wear anything but a suit or slacks and a dress shirt. In fact, she had begun to question whether he even owned any casual clothes. Apparently he did, and damned if he didn't look delicious in them.

When he heard her enter the room he looked up and said, "Good morning."

"Mornin'."

"There's coffee," he said.

"I can't. You know, the baby."

"I made decaf."

"Oh. Thanks."

"Sit down. I'll pour you a cup."

She took a seat across from his, while he got up and poured her coffee. She couldn't tell if she should be uncomfortable or not. She was having a tough time reading him.

He set a steaming cup of black coffee in front of her and asked, "Are you hungry? I could make eggs or something."

"I didn't know billionaire oil men cooked."

"They do if they're hungry and their house-keeper is running errands. Or if you don't trust my cooking, I could take you out."

"I think maybe we should just talk instead."

He sat across from her. "Okay, let's talk."

She sat there for a minute and realized, they

had so many things to cover, she wasn't even sure where to begin. "Where should we start?"

"Why don't we start with us."

She grimaced. She had really hoped that was the one part they wouldn't have to talk about. And she knew that as much as she wanted there to be, there was no "us."

"I think we both know that this has the potential to get very complicated," he said.

It already was. "Look," she said. "Last night was great, but it never should have happened. Things are just so…jumbled up. We let our emotions get the best of us."

He looked relieved. "I'm glad you feel that way."

She knew he would be. She was letting him off easy. Giving him an out. Of course he would take it.

"But I want us to be friends," he said.

The "let's still be friends" speech. How many times had she heard that one? She gazed into the inky depths of her cup, so he wouldn't see how much this was hurting her.

And let's face it, even if he suddenly decided that he wanted a wife, that he wanted *her,* she would never cut it as the future Mrs. Adam Blair. He was way out of her league. Not to mention that he was here, and she was in Peckins. It was an impossible situation.

"Katy?"

"We could be having a baby together. That means we're more or less stuck with each other."

He arched one brow. "You make it sound pretty awful."

Because for her it would be. For a while anyway. But it was imperative he didn't know that. Because then he would feel guilty, and things would get uncomfortable. That was the last thing she wanted.

She forced a smile. "That's not what I meant. And of course we'll be friends."

"After talking to Dr. Meyer, I think we have to face the fact that it probably is ours."

"I know I said that I wasn't ready for a child of my own, but now that it's a possibility...I could never just hand it over to you."

He reached across the table and curled his hands over hers. She wished he would stop doing that. Stop touching her. He was only making it harder. "Katy, I would *never* expect you to do that. If it's our baby, we'll figure out a way to make it work."

Our baby. Hearing him say that gave her shivers.

She pulled her hands from his, before she did something stupid, like throw herself in his arms and *beg* him to love her. To at least try.

"What about the surrogacy agreement?" she asked.

"Null and void, I guess. We'll have to work out some kind of custody agreement and child support. But I don't want you to worry. Financially, everything will be taken care of."

Custody and child support? What a nightmare.

"I don't want to wait for the birth for the DNA test," she told him. "I want to do the amnio. As soon as possible."

"The doctor said there are risks. Is it really that critical to know so soon?"

Not for him, maybe. But it was for her. "I need to know what to feel."

He frowned. "I don't understand."

"Either way, this is your baby. You're the father. But what am I? The baby's mother or just the aunt? I can't bear spending nine months thinking

I'm going to have my own child, only to find that I have no maternal rights."

"I guess I never thought of it like that. Of course we'll do the amnio."

And until then she would just have to try to stay partial, try not to get too attached. Just in case. Because having her heart broken again so soon would be more than even she could bear.

"I also think we shouldn't talk about this with anyone but the doctor," she told him. "Not until we get the results. I can't put my parents through that."

Although, ironically, they were in the same situation as Adam. Whether it was Becca's baby or Katy's, it was still their grandchild. Only Katy's dilemma was unique.

"Whatever you want," Adam said. "I know this isn't what either one of us signed on for, but we'll make this work, Katy. Everything will be okay."

Eventually, she hoped.

She looked up at the clock, saw how late it was getting and said, "I really need to get home."

"You don't have to run off."

Oh, no, she did. The longer she stayed here, the

more her heart hurt. "I have to get back to the ranch, and you probably have to get to work."

"I have been taking a lot of time off lately."

She took a swallow of coffee then got up and dumped what was left in the sink.

Adam got up, too. "I'll walk you out."

It was another scorcher, and she found herself looking forward to the cooler weather of autumn. She opened the truck door and turned to say goodbye, and Adam was right behind her. Startled, she stumbled backward and hit the front seat with the small of her back. He stepped closer, caging her in, and suddenly she couldn't breathe, couldn't think straight. And he knew it.

"One last kiss?" he asked, but he was already leaning in, taking charge.

No, no, please don't do this, she begged silently, but then his lips were on hers, and Lord help her, she couldn't deny him. His arms went around her, crushing her against the solid wall of his body. His fingers tangled in her hair. And she melted.

"Come back inside with me," he whispered against her lips. "Just one more time, and I promise I'll never ask again."

She wanted to, more than he would ever know.

But she couldn't. Her heart was already splitting in two. He thought they'd had really awesome, no-strings-attached sex. But the strings were there, invisible to the naked eye, and she had to back away, before she became hopelessly entangled.

Adam watched Katy drive away, feeling... conflicted. Which was not a familiar feeling. He didn't want her to leave, and at the same time, he knew it was for the best. He cared about Katy. And though she was trying to hide it, he could see that she had pretty strong feelings for him. The last thing he wanted to do was hurt her. Especially now.

"I hope you know what you're doing."

He spun around to find Celia standing in the front doorway watching him. "Your note said you were running errands."

"I was. Then I got home."

Great. "You could have said something."

"But then I wouldn't have been able to eavesdrop, would I?"

At least she wasn't shy about admitting it. "How long have you been here?"

She folded her arms across her chest. "Long enough."

Long enough to hear something that was putting that disapproving look on her face. The look that, since he was a small boy, always preceded a firm lecture.

He really wasn't in the mood.

"I assume you don't plan to marry her," she said.

"That would be a correct assumption. We don't even know for sure that the baby is hers."

"And if it is?"

He wouldn't marry her then, either.

She stared at him, tight-lipped.

"Don't do that," he said, walking past her into the house. "I'm not a kid any longer."

She slammed the door. "Then stop acting like one."

Wow, he hadn't seen her this angry in a long time. Not since the time he stole the headmaster's keys, took his Beamer for a spin, then crashed it into a tree. His father, whose attention he'd been trying to get, had been too busy to come get him, so he'd sent Celia. And boy was she pissed. Just like now.

And for what?

"I really don't see why you're so upset," he said.

"I'm upset because I like Katy, and you're breaking her heart."

"That's ridiculous." He walked to the kitchen and she followed him. This had nothing to do with Katy's heart. "She's understandably upset. It's a complicated situation."

"She's upset because she loves you, *estúpido*. And you're too much of a chicken to admit what you know is the truth."

He took a sip of his coffee, but it was cold, so he dumped it in the sink. When he turned back to her, she was staring at him. He sighed. "Okay, I'll bite. What *is* the truth?"

"That she could very well be the best thing that has ever happened to you! She's your soul mate."

An unexpected surge of emotion had him turning toward the window. "I buried my soul mate three years ago."

She stepped up behind him, touched his shoulder. "You buried your wife," she said softly, "but not your soul mate."

That wasn't the way he saw it.

"How long are you going to keep her up on a

pedestal, pretending everything was perfect? I cared for Becca, and I know you loved her in your own way, but you were never half as happy with her as you are with Katy. You have this light in your eyes when you talk about her, and you probably don't realize it, but you talk about her a lot. And when you're with her…it's just so obvious that you two are meant to be together."

Celia was obviously seeing things that weren't really there. It was no secret that she hadn't been crazy about the idea of him marrying Becca. She never thought they were a good match. But she had been good to Becca nonetheless. Even when Becca sometimes hadn't been so nice to her. Becca wanted to be his entire universe and she'd been jealous of his relationship with Celia.

And yes, they'd had difficult times, and marital troubles, and instead of facing them he'd buried himself in work instead. But that wasn't her fault. He hadn't given their marriage a chance to be better.

And if he had, if they'd had a perfect marriage and had been blissfully happy, losing her would have been even more unbearable.

"I won't bury another wife," he told Celia.

"You don't get to choose who you love. The question is whether or not you accept that love."

"I'm content with my life just the way it is, and when the baby is here, it will be perfect."

"You really believe that?"

"I *know* that." He looked at his watch. "Now, I need to get to work."

She frowned and shook her head, as if she was thoroughly disappointed in him. But the last thing he needed was her playing matchmaker.

Did he have feelings for Katy? Of course. Could he love her? Without a doubt, but that didn't mean he should allow it. He wouldn't make that mistake again.

Thirteen

Though he planned to hold off until their regular manager's meeting, Adam couldn't wait to announce his good news. And after speaking with the rest of the board of directors, it was agreed that the sooner he set things in motion, the better. Though it meant shuffling a few meetings around, he gathered everyone in his office later that afternoon.

"I have a bit of good news," he said, then added, "Personal news," gaining the rapt attention of everyone. "I'm going to be a father."

Emilio grinned, while Nathan and Jordan just looked stunned.

"I wasn't even aware you were seeing anyone. Much less seriously enough to father a child," Nathan said, obviously anticipating a public-relations nightmare on the horizon. "Tell me she isn't the daughter of anyone important. Or, God forbid, underage."

Adam laughed. Leave it to him to expect the worst. "There's no scandal here. It's mine and Rebecca's child."

Nathan blinked. "Oh."

Jordan looked confused. "How is that possible?"

Adam told them about the embryos, and Katy's offer to carry the baby. For now, that was all they needed to know.

A lot of backslapping and handshakes followed, but he wasn't finished yet.

"There's something else. Something I'll be announcing formally in a few months. But I wanted to tell you all first. After the baby is born, I'm stepping down as CEO of Western Oil."

Three mouths fell open in unison.

"Stepping down?" Nathan asked. "You live for this company."

"I'll still be on the board. I just won't be as

involved in the day-to-day operations. I want to be there for my child."

"Had you considered hiring a nanny?" Nathan asked.

"I could do that," Adam said. "But I promised myself a long time ago that when I had children, I would be there for them. Not a ghost, like my father. Especially since I'm raising this child on my own."

"Which raises the question, will you look outside the company for a replacement, or promote from within?" Emilio asked, getting to the heart of the matter.

"I've already spoken to the board. It was agreed that we would promote from within."

The three men exchanged glances. That meant that for the next eight months they would be under a veritable microscope, their every decision and act used to judge them. Three friends—two of them family—in competition for the brass ring. It had the potential to get very ugly. How they all handled the stress would be a determining factor to the board's decision.

"So who would you choose?" Nathan asked,

knowing that the board would most likely follow Adam's lead.

"I won't make a choice until the board votes," he told them. "Until then everyone has an equal shot at the position. In essence, my choice will depend on your performance for the next eight months."

"No pressure there," Jordan said wryly.

"This position *is* pressure," Adam told him. "And as you all know I have a lot vested in this company. We all do. If not for each one of you, it wouldn't be what it is today."

"I think we all know who will get it," Nathan said. "You and Emilio are good friends. He's obviously got the advantage."

"This is business," Adam said. "Friendship has nothing to do with it."

"Not to mention that I'm going to leave you guys in the dust," Jordan said smugly, with a smile that said he was as good as in. His brother glared, but was smart enough to keep his mouth shut.

"Any questions?" Adam asked, but everyone seemed pretty clear on the way things would be until the decision was made.

When the meeting was over, Emilio hung back. "I just wanted to say congratulations again. I know this is something you've wanted for a long time."

Adam gestured for him to close the door. He'd promised Katy he wouldn't tell anyone the truth, but Emilio was one of his closest friends. He knew he could trust him to keep their secret.

Emilio shut the door and sat back down.

"What I said about the baby being mine and Becca's, that might not be the case."

He frowned. "Whose is it, then?"

"Mine and Katy's."

"You slept with her?"

"The day the embryos were transferred the second time. The doctor says there's a five-to-one chance Katy's egg was fertilized."

Emilio shook his head and muttered something in Spanish. "Maybe this was inevitable."

Inevitable? "What do you mean?"

"A man doesn't talk about a woman constantly unless he's attracted to her."

Had he really talked about her so much that both Celia and Emilio took notice? Without even realizing it?

"What are you going to do now?" Emilio asked.

"The only thing we can do. Have a DNA test, and if it is Katy's, share custody."

"You won't marry her?"

Emilio had no business lecturing him on marriage. "I'm surprised you would even ask that. Especially when you're so against marriage."

Emilio shrugged. "I'm not the marrying type. You are."

He *was*. But not anymore. "You know damn well I'm never getting married again."

"I know you've said that."

"But you obviously don't believe it."

"I believe you have a responsibility to the child. And its mother."

"And if you were in my position? Would you ask her to marry you?"

"Of course."

Adam was stunned. "You don't believe in marriage."

"No, but in my culture it's a matter of pride for a man to take responsibility for his actions," he said, then added sheepishly, "And if I didn't, my mother would probably disown me."

"So you think I should marry her."

"What I think doesn't matter."

Then why all the unsolicited advice? What the hell was with everyone lately? First Celia, now Emilio?

"This is getting really complicated."

"You slept with your deceased wife's sister and you're having a baby. At what point did you think it *wouldn't* be complicated?"

He had a point.

"Look," Emilio said. "You've had a rough couple of years. I just think that you deserve to be happy." He looked at his watch and pushed himself up from his chair. "And speaking of being happy, I have a date with a lovely *older* woman."

"Older?"

"My mother," he said with a grin.

"You have my sympathies." Monthly trips to the opera was one part of his marriage Adam didn't miss. Becca insisted they keep box seats. He used the time to either check email on his phone, or take a nap.

Emilio chuckled. "Not all men hate opera."

No, but he was betting more than half were only there for their wives. Although he had come to suspect that Becca favored the social aspect of the experience over the actual performance. She was big on flaunting their wealth, and always obsessed with wearing clothes from whichever up-and-coming designer was in favor at the time. She routinely spent the entire day in the salon getting her hair and nails and makeup fixed. He could never figure out why she couldn't be content to just be herself. Like Katy.

He did not just think that. Maybe he *was* too preoccupied with her.

Emilio was at the door when Adam asked, "Before you go, can I ask you a question?"

"Of course."

"Before Becca got sick, did I seem happy?"

Emilio frowned. "I'm not sure what you mean."

"Did you think we had a good marriage?"

He considered that, as though choosing his words carefully. "I recall thinking that if you were happy, you would have spent less time at work, and more with your wife."

"You work as much as I do."

"But I don't have a wife at home."

Another good point.

"Out of curiosity, why do you ask?"

"Celia said something this morning…" He

shrugged. "You know what, never mind. Have fun tonight."

Emilio looked like he wanted to say more, but he knew Adam well enough not to push.

When he was gone, Adam glanced at the phone. Talking about Katy made him want to pick it up and call. She'd text messaged him earlier to say that she had gotten back home safely, so he really had no reason to call her. Maybe all he wanted was to hear her voice.

Which was exactly why he didn't do it.

Adam managed to hold out a week before he stumbled across a legitimate excuse to call Katy. He was reading an article on the internet about prenatal DNA testing, and a safer, less invasive method was mentioned.

He called her cell but it went straight to voice, so he tried the ranch phone instead. Katy's mom answered.

"Well, hello, Adam. What a pleasant surprise. How have you been?"

"Good. Busy."

"You know, we didn't get a chance to congratulate you. We were so pleased to hear that it worked the second time. I did some reading on the subject online and it sounds as though you and Katy were quite lucky."

Not as much as she might think.

"Is she there?" he asked.

"She's out running errands for her father, but she has her cell with her. Do you have the number?"

"I tried her cell but it went right to voice mail." He hoped the errands didn't involve any heavy lifting. She had to be careful not to overexert herself.

"There are a lot of holes in the service out here. She was probably driving through a dead zone."

What was the point of even having a cell phone if there was no reception? What if she got into an accident, or broke down? He would have to look into getting her a satellite phone.

"Don't forget, we still owe you that supper," she told him. "We'd just love it if you came up to see us. It's only right we celebrate together. We could make a day of it."

"I'd like that," he said, surprised by the realization that he actually meant it.

"You're welcome anytime. You know we don't

stand on formality here. You just jump in your car and head up whenever the mood strikes."

"I'll do that."

"You're family, Adam. Don't ever forget that."

He had a sudden and unexpected lump in his throat. Her parents had every reason to think the worst of him, yet they still considered him one of them.

It was sad that Becca never understood what an extraordinary family she had, and he regretted not insisting she make more of an effort to keep in touch.

He regretted a lot of things about their marriage, and only recently had he begun to realize that.

"When Katy gets in could you tell her I called?"

"Will do, Adam. You take care."

He hung up and tried her cell again, this time leaving a message. "Hey, Katy, it's me. I found some interesting information about DNA testing that I want to discuss with you. Call me when you get this."

He answered a few emails while he waited for her to call him back. But after an hour passed, he began to wonder if she'd gotten his message. He dialed her cell, once again getting her voice mail.

"Me again," he said. "I just wanted to make sure you got my last message. Call me."

She was probably on the road, he figured, and wouldn't check her messages until she got home. Which was fine, since she shouldn't be driving and talking on her phone at the same time anyway. No point in taking chances.

He immersed himself in work, and before he knew it, it was nearly five o'clock. Katy hadn't called yet, but he was sure she had to be home by now. He tried her cell, but again it went straight to voice.

He dialed the ranch, and her mother answered again. "She's here, Adam, but she's out in the north pasture with her father. As soon as she gets inside I'll tell her you called. It shouldn't be more than an hour."

He waited one and a half, then he got caught up in an overseas call that ate another hour. When he was finished Bren buzzed him.

"Ms. Huntley called."

"Why didn't you tell me?" he snapped, and realized he'd just bit her head off unjustly. She had strict instructions that unless it was a dire emergency she was not to interrupt overseas calls.

"Sorry," he said. "Long day."

He picked up the phone and called Katy back again.

"You mean she didn't call you?" her mother said, sounding surprised. "I gave her your message."

"No, she did. But I was on an overseas call. Is she there now?"

"No. She left about ten minutes ago. She went to see a movie with her friend Willy."

Willy? "Willy Jenkins?"

"That's right."

He felt his hackles rise. She was with Willy "Friends-with-Benefits" Jenkins? The idea of what they might do after the film made his blood pressure skyrocket.

"I'll probably be asleep when she gets in, but I'll leave a message that you called."

Meaning she was expecting Katy to be late. "I'd appreciate that," he told her, jaw tense. He hung up and shoved himself back from his desk. As long as she was pregnant with *his* child she had no business sleeping with *anyone*. Who knows what kind of diseases or viruses this Willy person could have contracted? The way she made it sound, he wasn't one to turn down a casual roll in the hay. He could have slept with dozens of women.

He distinctly recalled that when she offered to do this for him, she agreed to practice abstinence.

The only exception to that particular rule was if the man she was sleeping with was *him*.

After playing phone tag for the better part of the next day, Katie finally got a hold of Adam around seven. Her parents were outside so she curled up on the couch with the cordless phone.

Though she had tried hard to keep him off her mind, she'd missed him. Missed hearing his voice.

"Hi, it's me," she said when he answered.

"Well, you're a tough woman to get a hold of," he said sharply.

She was so taken aback she was speechless. And hurt. They hadn't talked in almost a week, and when they finally did he was a jerk. He was clearly upset with her, but she couldn't imagine what she'd done.

"I've been calling you for two days," he said. "I guess you've been busy."

"Busy?"

"Going on dates with Willy Jenkins."

Dates? Is that what this was about? Her mom must have mentioned she went to the movies last night when she talked to him. Although she would hardly call it a date. "You have a problem with me going to the show with a friend?"

"I do if you're sleeping with him."

Sleeping with him? Where the heck had that come from? Her mom sure hadn't told him *that*. "Who told you I was sleeping with him?"

"You did."

"I did? When?"

"That day in the coffee shop. You said you were 'friends with benefits.'"

Yes, but that was years ago, and… Oh, good Lord. She slapped a hand over her mouth to stifle a giggle.

Was he jealous? Of *Willy?*

The billionaire oil man was threatened by a lowly ranch hand? Adam must have been sitting around all day stewing in his own juices.

It was such a ridiculous notion, and he had himself in such a lather, she couldn't resist poking the lion with a stick.

"What makes you think it's any of your business *who* I sleep with?" she asked him.

"As long as you're pregnant with my child, it's my business."

"How do you figure?"

"We had an agreement that you would practice abstinence while you were pregnant."

They did? She didn't recall agreeing to that. But since she'd had no plans to sleep with *anyone*—not even him—it never seemed relevant anyway. "So I should be practicing abstinence, unless I'm having sex with you? Is that it?"

There was a pause, then he said, "That's different."

Behind her someone cleared their throat, and she snapped her head around to find her mom standing in the kitchen doorway. The woman was stealthy as a damned cat. And it was clear, by her expression, that she'd heard what Katy said about sleeping with Adam.

Well, damn it all to hell.

Fourteen

"Adam, I need to call you back," Katy said.

"Why?" he demanded.

"Because I do."

"We need to discuss this," he barked, like he was issuing an executive order.

"I know we do. It'll just be a few minutes."

"What's so important you can't talk to me right now?"

At the end of her patience, she said, "Willy is here for a quickie, that's what!"

She hung up on him and dropped the phone on the couch beside her.

Her mom stood in the kitchen doorway, arms folded, shaking her head. "That was real mature."

Not one of her finer moments, but he was sort of asking for it.

The phone immediately began to ring. Her mom walked over to the couch, picked it up and answered. "Well, hello, Adam." She paused then said, "She's not feeling too well. Morning sickness, I'm afraid."

Another pause, then she said, "Yes, I know it's not morning. They just call it that, but it can happen anytime of day. I'll have her call you back when it passes."

She hung up and sat down beside Katy.

"I fell hard and fast, just like you said I would," Katy admitted. "So go ahead, say I told you so."

"Would it make you feel better if I did?"

She sighed and collapsed back against the couch cushions. "Probably not."

"Are you...*seeing* him?"

"He didn't want me." She shrugged, suddenly on the verge of tears. "What else is new, right?"

"Oh, honey." She gathered Katy in her arms and hugged her.

"I guess I should have listened to you."

"At least now I know why you've been moping

around for a week." She paused, then asked, "Did he…seduce you?"

"He was a perfect gentleman," she admitted, as if she wasn't ashamed enough. "This was my fault. I don't know what I was thinking. I guess I *wasn't* thinking."

"It'll be easier after you have the baby. You won't have to see him at all if you don't want to."

Now that her mom knew about the affair, not fessing up to the rest of it felt like lying. "Actually, I might be stuck seeing him a lot. For at least the next nineteen years."

"What do you mean?"

"There's a pretty good chance that my own egg was fertilized."

She braced for the fireworks, but instead her mom hugged her tighter. "Oh, Katy. Why didn't you say something?"

"I thought you would be angry. And I was embarrassed that I screwed things up so badly."

"How does Adam feel about this?"

"He's been wonderful. Besides breaking my heart, but that isn't his fault. I know how you and Daddy feel about him, but he's not the person you think he is. Rebecca lied to us, Mom. About a lot of things."

"Katy—"

"I know you don't want to believe it. I didn't, either. But Adam told me things, and he has no reason to lie."

"I don't find that so hard to believe," she said, sounding sad.

"We don't have to tell Daddy about the baby, do we?" Katy asked.

"Your father and I don't keep secrets."

"He's going to be furious. And he's going to want to kill Adam."

"Give him a little credit. He may be upset at first, but he'll be reasonable. I do think it will be easier to swallow coming from me."

She was so relieved she felt limp. "When are you going to tell him?"

"I'll talk to him tonight, when we go up to bed. That way he'll have all night to mull it over before he talks to you."

She threw her arms around her mother and hugged her. "Thank you. For being so understanding. I thought you would be so disappointed in me."

"Oh, sweetheart, you've been the best daughter a mother could ask for. It would take an awful lot to disappoint me."

Katy rested her head on her mother's shoulder, breathed in the scent of her perfume. Avon Odyssey. She'd worn the same fragrance as long as Katy could remember. It was familiar and comforting.

"So, does Adam know how you feel about him?"

"What's the point? Even if he felt the same way, it would never work. We're too different."

"Different how?"

"He's rich and sophisticated, and I'm not."

"So, you think he's better than you?"

"Not better, but we want different things out of life. Not to mention that he's in El Paso. And I'm happy right here, where I am." She sat back and looked at her mother. "Aren't you the one who told me that he's not like us?"

"I guess I did." She touched Katy's cheek. "I just don't like to see my baby unhappy. And like you said, maybe he's not the man we thought he was. He must be pretty special if you fell for him."

"Well, it's all a moot point because Adam said himself that he'll never get married again. And even if he did, if he wanted me, I would always feel as though I was competing with Rebecca. I don't think she had a clue how lucky she was."

"Probably not. Your sister took a lot of things for granted."

She sat snuggled up to her mom, like she had when she was little, and found herself wishing she could go back to those days. When things were so much less complicated, and her life actually made sense.

"You should probably call Adam back," her mom said.

Yeah, and she should probably apologize for the "quickie" remark. In all fairness, if their roles were reversed, she wouldn't be too keen on the idea of the mother of her child sleeping around.

It wasn't Adam's fault that she'd fallen for him, so it wasn't right to take out her frustrations on him.

"I'll call him right now."

Her mom gave her one last firm squeeze, then got up from the couch. Katy hit Redial, expecting Adam to be fuming by now, but when he answered he sounded humbled.

"Are you okay?" he asked.

"I'm fine."

"I owe you an apology," he said, totally stunning her. "I overreacted. I'm used to being in charge, being in control, and with you so far away, I'm feeling a little...well, helpless, I guess."

She knew that hadn't been easy for him to admit. "I'm sorry, too. That remark about Willy was uncalled for. Of course you have every right to be concerned. And for the record, I'm not sleeping with him or anyone else. Nor do I intend to."

"I don't suppose you would reconsider moving here until the baby is born."

Good Lord, what a nightmare that would be. As if this wasn't complicated and heartbreaking enough. "I can't, Adam."

"Just thought I would ask."

"And, just so you know, I wasn't sick. My mom overheard what I said about us sleeping together, and I could tell she wanted an explanation."

"How much did you tell her?"

"Everything."

She could practically feel him grimacing. "I thought you wanted to wait until we knew for sure."

"I did, but not telling her started to feel like lying. And she took it surprisingly well."

"What about your dad?"

"She's telling him tonight. He may not take it so well."

"He doesn't happen to keep firearms around?"

She smiled. "Yeah, but he hasn't pulled his rifle on anyone since I was sixteen and he caught me behind the stable kissing one of the ranch hands."

"You are kidding. Right?"

"Nope. Not only did the guy get fired on the spot, I think he had to go change his shorts."

"I guess I should watch my back, then."

"Nah. If my dad was going to take you down it would be in the chest. Or if he really wanted you to suffer, the gut."

"Now you *are* kidding," he said, but he sounded a little nervous.

She laughed. "Yeah, I'm kidding."

"So, you've been feeling okay?"

"I've been feeling great."

They eased into a conversation about her pregnancy, and he told her about the test he'd read of on the internet. They made plans to bring it up at her next appointment in three weeks. They ended up talking for almost an hour. She lay in bed later, replaying the conversation over and over, wishing things were different. Both anticipating and dreading her doctor appointment. Sometimes she missed Adam so much, the feeling sat like a stone in her chest. She knew seeing him face-to-face would only make it worse. Yet she longed to be close to him again. And she was terrified that if he got too close, if he wanted to make love again, she wouldn't be able to tell him no.

She tossed and turned all night and woke so late the next morning she missed breakfast, but Elvie kept some scrambled eggs and bacon warm for her. After she ate she went searching and found her mom in the chicken coop.

"Sorry I slept in."

"That's okay. Your body is changing. You need more rest than before. I used to get exhausted in my first few months."

"Is there anything you need me to do before I

lock myself in the office?" It was her day to do the payroll and order supplies.

"Nothing I can think of."

Katy turned to leave and her mom added, "I talked with your dad last night."

Katy's heart gave a resounding thud. She had completely forgotten that she was going to break the news. "So, what did he say?"

"He said he sort of had the feeling something was up with the two of you," her father said from behind her. Katy swung around to find him leaning in the coop doorway. "And he said that while he'd prefer to see you married and settled down, a baby is a blessing. No matter whose it is."

"Thank you, Daddy," she said, and all of a sudden she was on the verge of tears.

Then he came over and hugged her and she did start crying.

She felt terrible for thinking he would be angry, and expecting the worst. As far as parents went, hers were pretty darned wonderful. It made her wonder, as she had so many times before, how could Becca have taken them for granted?

As long as she lived, it was a mistake she would never repeat.

* * *

The day of Katy's appointment couldn't come fast enough.

Adam told himself it was because he was eager to learn about the baby's progress, but the truth was, he'd missed her. Since their phone conversation, when he'd accused her of sleeping with her friend Willy, they'd been talking a lot more often. Usually in the evenings, after he left work and she finished her chores. He had never been much of a talker. He was more the silent-observer type, but that turned out not to be a problem, because Katy did enough talking for the both of them. And the more they talked, he found himself opening up to her.

It was astounding how different she and Becca really were. While Becca had been complex and at times intractable, Katy was so…uncomplicated. And honest. If she said something, she meant it. There were none of the games women seemed to like to play. He found himself calling more often, making up excuses to talk to her, just so he could hear her voice.

Though he'd known many women in his life, he'd never actually been friends with one. Sadly, he realized, not even Becca. They used to talk when they were first dating, but now he wondered if she was only telling him what she thought he wanted to hear. Katy in contrast didn't pull any punches. If she felt strongly about something, she wasn't afraid to speak her mind. At times quite passionately. But he liked that she challenged him. Because in all honesty, given his position of power in the corporate sector, not many people stood up to him.

He considered her more of an equal than most of his "rich" friends and colleagues.

The day of the appointment, when Reece pulled the limo into the lot at the fertility clinic and saw her truck already parked there, Adam experienced an anticipation that he'd not felt in a very long time. He didn't even wait for Reece to get out and open his door. And when he walked inside and saw her standing near the elevator, something deep inside of him seemed to…settle. Followed promptly by the yearning to pull her into his arms and hold her.

She smiled brightly when she saw him, her skin glowing with good health and happiness. Just the way he imagined a pregnant woman should look.

She was dressed in her girls' clothes, and though she looked sexy as hell, he knew she would look even better wearing nothing at all. But the last thing either of them needed was to complicate this situation, and sleeping with her would do just that.

But damn, what he wouldn't give to take a quick nibble of her plump, rosy lips.

"Hi, stranger," she said as he approached her, rising up to give him a quick hug and a peck on the cheek. It took all his willpower not to turn his head so it was his lips she kissed instead. There was an energy that crackled between them. The same sensation of awareness he'd felt when they kissed the first time.

"You look fantastic," he said.

"Thanks. I feel great. My friend Missy is jealous because by this point in all four of her pregnancies she was sick as a dog."

The elevator opened and they stepped inside. He touched her back, to guide her, and electricity seemed to arc between them. And he knew, from the soft breathy sound she made, the slight widening of her eyes, that she felt it, too.

When they signed in at the doctor's office they

were called back immediately to an exam room. Adam waited in the hall while she changed into a gown, and he was only in the room a minute or two when Dr. Meyer knocked.

"So how have you been feeling?" he asked Katy. "Any morning sickness?"

"None at all. I feel great. A little tired sometimes, but I just go to bed earlier."

The doctor smiled. "Sounds like a reasonable solution. You've been taking the vitamins I prescribed?"

"Every morning. And our cook has been filling me up on vegetables and whole grains."

"Excellent."

He asked her a few more questions, then took her blood pressure and pulse.

"I need to do an internal exam," he said, looking from Adam to Katy, as if he wasn't sure Adam would be staying or not. And frankly neither was Adam. But Katy smiled and said, "That's fine."

It wasn't as if he hadn't been up close and personal with every conceivable inch of her body anyway, but the doctor was still very discreet.

"Everything seems to be progressing well," he

said when he was finished. "Why don't you get dressed and meet me in my office."

After he stepped out of the room, Adam said, "Thanks for letting me stay."

"I'll bet seeing that makes you pretty happy to be a guy," she joked.

"Men have their own indignities to endure," he said, but spared her the gory details. "I'll wait in the hall for you."

Katy emerged a few minutes later and they walked down the hall to Dr. Meyer's office.

"Do you have any questions for me?" he asked when they were seated.

"We've been reading up on DNA testing," Adam told him, and asked about different options. His opinion was that if they wanted to do the test as soon as possible, the safest way would be through amnio.

"I have a question, too," Katie said. "My mom was telling me how fast her labors were, and since I'm two hours away, I'm wondering what that could mean for me. So far my pregnancy has been just like hers were. I'm afraid that if I go into labor and have to drive all the way to El Paso, I might give birth in the truck."

"I didn't realize you lived so far from here," the doctor said, looking concerned. "Do you have a regular ob-gyn closer to home you could see?"

"I've been seeing Dr. Hogue since I was twelve, and he delivered both me and my sister."

"I know Dr. Hogue. He's a very competent physician."

Adam wasn't sure he liked that. "Shouldn't she be seeing you?"

"Honestly, as long as her pregnancy remains uneventful—and I have no reason to believe it won't—I see no reason why Katy shouldn't see her regular physician. I'm sure he'll have no problem keeping me apprised of her progress."

Meaning Adam would be driving to Peckins for her appointments instead of Katy coming here.

"Are you upset?" Katy asked him when they left the office and walked down the hall to the elevator.

"Not upset. I wish you would have discussed this with me first."

"I know, and I would have, but it was something my mom brought up this morning before I left. And while I like Dr. Meyer, I think I'll be more comfortable seeing Doc Hogue. He knows me."

Adam could object, and insist she see Meyer, but why? What was his justification?

It would be an inconvenience for him. Though no more than it was for her. And since she was the pregnant one, wasn't it safer if he did the traveling? And she had a valid point about getting to the hospital. "If that's what you want, then of course."

She took his hand and squeezed it, smiling up at him. "Thank you, Adam."

Their eyes met, then locked, and he felt it like a fist to his gut. His palm buzzed, then went hot where it touched hers. He wanted to kiss her. No, he *needed* to. And he was 99 percent sure she was thinking the same thing.

As if caught in a magnetic pull their bodies began to move in closer, her chin tipped upward, and his head dipped....

Then the damned elevator door slid open and people stepped out. Katy jerked back, breaking the spell.

He cursed silently as he followed her on and they rode it down to the first floor. They walked

though the lobby and out the door. It was over-
cast, and thunder rumbled in the distance. The
weathermen had been predicting rain.

"Sounds like there's a storm headed this way,"
he said.

"I better get going," Katy said. "So I beat it
home."

"But you just got here. I thought we could spend
some time together."

"I really have to go."

Reece pulled up to the curb to meet him, but
Adam gestured for him to wait, and followed
Katy to where her truck was parked.

"You could at least let me take you to lunch."

"I don't think so." She seemed in an awful
hurry to leave, and she wouldn't look at him.

He took her by the arm and turned her to face
him. "Katy, what's wrong?"

"I just really need to go."

"Why?"

She glanced around, like she worried someone might be listening. "Because you almost just
kissed me, and if I stay, you *will* kiss me."

"Would that be so terrible?"

"Yes, because after you kiss me you'll make up

some stupid excuse why I should come to your house, and I will, because at this point my brain will have completely shorted out. And we won't be there thirty seconds before we're naked and… well, you know the rest."

"Would *that* really be so terrible?"

"I'm not a yo-yo. You can't say one minute that it would complicate things, then try to jump me the next. It's not fair."

She was right. He was sending mixed signals like crazy. He cared for her. More than any other woman he'd been involved with, maybe even Becca, but this relationship had no future. Not a romantic one anyway. To let himself love her, to care that much, would make it that much more unbearable if he ever lost her.

Though he wished it were possible, he couldn't give her what she wanted. What she deserved. A man who would love her, and marry her.

"You're right. I'm sorry."

A bolt of lightning arced across the sky to the south.

"I really have to go," she said.

"You'll call me and let me know when you make your appointment."

"Of course."

"And let me know that you got home safely."

"I will." She hesitated, then rose up to press a kiss to his cheek, lingering a second before she turned and climbed in the truck, and as he watched her back out and drive away, he could swear he saw tears in her eyes.

Fifteen

As soon as Katy got home from El Paso she called and made an appointment with Doc Hogue, then she texted Adam with the date and time, because frankly she was feeling too emotional to talk to him. It took everything in her not to sob all the way home. The way he looked at her…for a minute she let herself believe that he wanted her. As close as they had become lately, she thought he was going to tell her that he'd made a mistake, that he loved her.

Why did she keep doing this to herself? Even if he did love her, there was no rational way to make it work. They could try a long-distance relationship, but that would only last so long before they grew apart. She'd seen it happen before to friends who had boyfriends in the rodeo and the military.

When she chose to be with a man, she wanted be *with* him. Not one hundred and fifty miles away. Not that she could be with a man who didn't want to be with her. But she was happy that she and the father of her child—if it *was* her child—would be good friends. Still, she was almost relieved when he called her a week before the doctor appointment to say that he had to fly out of the country and wouldn't make it back till two days after her appointment.

"It's imperative that I go," he told her.

"It's okay," she assured him. "Things happen. Besides, it's only my third month. I seriously doubt anything exciting will happen."

"I wanted to meet the doctor."

"So you'll meet him next month."

But next month didn't happen, either. Two days before her appointment Adam caught a nasty flu virus.

"You sound terrible," she said when he called to tell her, dousing her disappointment.

"I feel terrible," he croaked, his throat so raw and scratchy he could only speak in a coarse whisper.

"Do you have a fever?"

"One hundred and one. Celia won't let me out of bed and she's been force-feeding me chicken soup."

"Good. It sounds like what you need is rest."

"I'm sorry, Katy," he rasped.

"For what?"

"I feel terrible for missing another appointment. Not to mention the amnio. I wanted to be there with you."

And she had wanted him there. She didn't like feeling that she was in this alone. But he couldn't help that she was sick.

"I've heard it's really not that big of a deal. They'll numb me so I won't feel a thing. And, no offense, but I wouldn't want to go anywhere near you right now. The last thing I need is the flu. Just take care of yourself and you'll be better in time for the next appointment."

Her mom went with her to her appointment, and after her checkup, it was off to the hospital for the amnio—which really wasn't all that bad.

Doc Hogue had already warned her that it usually took six to eight weeks to get the results—in some cases even longer, and she knew the waiting would be torture.

When she called Adam to tell him the test went well, he sounded relieved. "Nothing will stop me from making the next appointment. I promise."

She hoped that was true. And not just because she wanted to see him, but things were progressing faster than she'd anticipated. Her mom had always said that she started showing early in her pregnancies, so Katy shouldn't have been surprised when, in the last week of her fourth month, she woke up one morning and couldn't fasten her jeans.

"Isn't that supposed to happen?" Adam asked when she called him later that night to complain. "And didn't you tell me that you're not worried about the physical repercussions of pregnancy."

"I don't care about that," she told him. "But there's nothing more I hate than shopping!"

He laughed and called her "unique."

Delaying the inevitable, she wore her jeans with the button unfastened, but after a couple more weeks, when she couldn't get the zipper up more than an inch, and the buttons on her shirts were stretched to the limit, her mom dragged her to the maternity shop for a new wardrobe.

With her next appointment only a week away, Katy felt torn in two. On one hand, she was anxious to see Adam, on the other, she was dreading it. They talked on the phone almost daily now, but seeing him face-to-face…she was afraid it would be a stark reminder of everything she couldn't have. Would *never* have. And though she had never come right out and told Adam how she felt, she was pretty sure he already knew. She also knew that if he was going to have a change of heart, he'd have had it by now. Losing his mother, then Becca, had done something to him. It had cut him so deeply she didn't think he would ever completely heal. He would never come right out and say it—he was too tough for that—but she knew he was afraid of being hurt again.

The Friday before her five-month checkup, Katy had finished up in the office for the day and was taking an afternoon nap when she woke to the sound of her mom's voice. She stood in the bedroom doorway.

"Wake up, honey. We have a visitor."

She sat up and yawned, rubbing her eyes. "Who?"

"Come down and see for yourself," she said, wearing a smile that made Katy suspect she was up to something.

Katy rolled out of bed and peeked out the window. There was a sporty little red car parked in front of the house. Who did they know who drove a sports car? She stretched to look out toward the barn and saw her father standing by the fence with a man Katy didn't recognize. Not from the back anyway at this distance. He was tall and broad-shouldered, wearing jeans, cowboy boots, a plaid flannel shirt and a black Stetson.

Puzzled, and anxious to meet the mystery man, she quickly dragged a comb through her sleep-matted hair and brushed her teeth.

She grabbed a sweater and headed downstairs, and as she glanced in the family room on her way out the front door she noticed a duffel bag next to the sofa. Whoever it was, it looked as though they were there for an extended stay. Maybe it was some long-lost cousin or uncle that she didn't know about.

She stepped out onto the porch, checking the car out as she walked past. The plates were Texas, but the car looked totally unfamiliar. And very expensive.

So it was a *rich* long-lost relative.

She crossed the yard to where her father stood with the mystery man, and he must have heard her coming because he suddenly turned in her direction. "There you are, Katy! Look who came to visit."

The man beside him turned, his head lowered so that his face was hidden by the brim of his hat. Then he lifted his chin, and when his face came into view, her heart did a somersault with a triple twist.

"Hello, Katy," Adam said.

Her first instinct was to throw herself into his arms and just hold him, but she restrained herself. Especially with her dad standing there. "What are you doing here? Our appointment isn't until Tuesday."

"I figured if I came early I would be guaranteed not to miss it this time. And your mom is always telling me I should come and stay for a few days. So here I am."

"Well," her dad said, looking from her to Adam. She could tell he was wary of Adam's presence, but he restrained himself from butting in. "I better head in and…see how dinner is coming along."

They both knew that the only part of dinner he ever participated in was eating it, and he was just making an excuse to leave them alone. But she was grateful.

When he was gone, Adam looked her up and down, eyes wide, and said, "Wow, you look…"

"Pregnant?" she finished for him.

He grinned, and it was so adorable her knees actually went weak. She'd missed seeing him smile. Missed everything about him. "I was going to say fantastic. Pregnancy definitely agrees with you."

She laid a hand on her rounded belly. "Doc Hogue said he's never had a patient who took to it so well. If it wasn't for my belly getting bigger, and the fact that some days I need an afternoon nap, I wouldn't even know that I was pregnant."

He nodded to her belly. "Can I feel?"

This was the part she dreaded. Well, one of the parts. He talked a lot about being anxious to touch her belly, and feel the baby move, and she knew darned well what happened when he put his hands on her. But she couldn't tell him no. Not when it meant so much to him.

"Sure," she said, trying to sound casual, when in reality her heart had begun to pound.

His hand was so big it practically dwarfed her tiny bump, and the warmth of his palm seeped through her shirt to warm her skin. "Have you felt the baby move?"

"Little flutters, but the book says those could just be muscle spasms. No kicks yet. But Doc Hogue said probably soon."

The feel of his hand on her belly was making her go all soft inside, and the energy building between them was reaching a critical level. She knew if she didn't back away soon she was going to do something really dumb, like throw her arms around his neck and kiss him, but Adam didn't give her a chance. His arms went around her, tentatively, as if he thought she might object to being held, and said, "I missed you, Katy."

She couldn't have fought it if she wanted to. She wrapped her arms around him and squeezed, tucking her head under his chin, breathing him in. "Me, too."

It was wonderful, and awful, because she managed to fall in love with him all over again. Not that she'd ever really stopped. But being apart for so long made her forget a little.

What if she *never* got over him?

The dinner bell started clanging and her mom called from the house, "Come on, you two. Time to eat!"

Though she didn't want to, Katy let go of Adam, and decided right then that there would be no more hugging and touching while he was here. It seemed he could turn his feelings on and off like a lightbulb, but for her it wasn't so easy. A few more days of this and her heart might never recover.

Something very weird was happening.

In the past, whenever Becca brought Adam over it was always awkward, the conversation stilted. Probably because Becca herself was so uncomfortable, as if being back home would rub off on her somehow and tarnish the new life she'd built with Adam. But now, everyone was happy and relaxed and seemed to genuinely enjoy each other's company.

After supper, while her dad took Adam out to the stables, Katy and her mom sat out on the porch swing.

"As much as I hate admitting I'm wrong," her mom said, "You were right about Adam. He's a good man. Maybe if your sister had been more comfortable here, he would have been, too."

"I've given up on trying to figure out why Becca did the things she did. Maybe if she'd lived, she would have eventually come around."

"Maybe," her mom said. They were quiet for several minutes, then she said off-handedly, "I noticed Adam couldn't keep his eyes off of you at dinner."

Katy had noticed that, too. Adam sat across from her, and every time she looked up from her plate he was watching her. And each time their eyes met she would feel this funny zing through her nervous system, and her heart would skip a beat. She'd barely been able to choke her dinner down. "What are you suggesting?"

Her mom shrugged. "Only that a man doesn't

look at a woman that way if he doesn't care about her."

Whether or not Adam cared about her wasn't in question. "But for me, that just isn't enough. I want the whole package. I deserve that. And, Adam, well, he's not available."

"Things change."

"Not this."

She might have argued further but Adam and her dad walked up, putting the conversation to an abrupt end.

They all sat out on the porch and watched the sunset until ten, when a chill set in the air. It was hard to believe it was fall already. The time seemed to fly by lately.

Her parents settled in front of the television to watch their favorite sitcom and her mom told Katy, "Why don't you get Adam settled in the blue room." When Katy cut her eyes sharply her way, she added, "It's the nicer of the two."

It was also right next door to, and shared a bathroom with, her own room. The green room was at least across the hall. Although, if he were staying with the men in the bunk house it would be too close as far as she was concerned.

Her mom wasn't trying to set them up, was she? Did she think proximity would make Adam change his mind? She wanted Katy to be happy, but she was making her miserable instead.

"This way," she told Adam, leading him up the stairs. He grabbed his duffel and followed her up. The heavy thud of his boots on the steps seemed to vibrate up through the balls of her feet to twang every single one of her nerves.

As soon as she hit the top step Sylvester darted out from his hiding spot behind the artificial palm tree and tried to wrap himself around her legs, so she toed him out of the way.

"The homicidal cat," Adam said.

"Homicidal?"

"He did that to me the last time I was here. I almost fell down the stairs."

"He can't help it. He got kicked in the head by a horse a few years back and he hasn't been right since. He mostly just stays up here and hides."

"And opens doors," Adam said with a grin, and she didn't have to ask what he meant. If it hadn't been for Sylvester opening her bedroom door, Adam never would have seen her naked, and maybe this entire mess might have been avoided.

She doubted it, though. With sexual attraction like theirs, sleeping with him had been inevitable.

"Here it is," she said, stepping into the spare room. "I know it isn't the Ritz, but the linens are fresh and there are clean towels in the bathroom cabinet. But if you flush the toilet and it keeps running just jiggle the handle and that should fix it."

The door snapped shut behind her and she whirled around to find Adam leaning against it. He had a look in his eyes, as if he was about ten seconds from devouring her.

Oh, Lord, give me strength.

"Don't look at me like that," she said.

His duffel landed with a thud on the floor beside him. "Like what?"

"Like I'm the main course on the buffet table."

He grinned. "Is that how I look?"

"I can't, Adam." But she wanted to. She wanted to slide her hands under his T-shirt, up his wide, muscular chest. She wanted to feel his bare skin against hers.

He took a step closer and her heart started to hammer. "I was just going to ask if I could feel the baby, that's all."

She didn't believe him for a second. Once he got his hands on her, her belly wasn't the only thing he would touch. And she would probably let him, because she wanted him so much she could hardly see straight.

"Maybe tomorrow," she told him. "I'm going to turn in for the night."

"It's barely ten."

"And I have to be up at five."

"How about a kiss goodnight, then?"

Why was he doing this to her? "I don't think so."

"Why?"

At the end of her rope, she asked, "Adam, what do you want from me?"

He shrugged. "I just...*want* you."

Isn't that the way it always was? They wanted her...until they didn't any longer. Well, she wanted forever, and he wasn't a forever kind of man. Not anymore. "That's not enough for me."

His expression was grim. "You want more."

"I *deserve* it."

"You do. And I'm being selfish." He opened the bedroom door. "I'm sorry. I'll back off."

"Do you need anything before I turn in?"

He shook his head. But as she walked past him to the door he caught her arm and pulled her to him. And heaven help her, she couldn't resist wrapping her arms around him.

Though it was packed with emotion, there was nothing sexual about the embrace. He just held her, and she held him. But it wasn't any less heartbreaking.

"I wish I could be what you need," he whispered against her hair.

She nodded, because if she tried to speak she would probably start blubbering. Besides, they'd already said all they needed to say.

Since he'd popped in unannounced, Adam felt it was only fair to do his share of work while he was visiting, so when Gabe invited him to ride along while he repaired fence posts, he went with him. It was tiresome, backbreaking work, but it felt good to be out in the fresh air and not cooped up in an office behind a desk for a change. Since Becca's death he'd become something of a shut-in. Now he was even thinking it was time to start living again.

They had finished replacing several busted

fence posts when Katy's mom brought them lunch on horseback. Thick barbequed beef sandwiches, a plastic bowl full of potato salad and cold sodas. They sat in the truck bed and ate. Adam was so famished he wolfed down two sandwiches and a huge pile of salad.

"Don't they feed you in El Paso?" Gabe asked with a wry grin.

"I don't get this hungry sitting behind a desk," he admitted.

"Out here you earn your appetite. When I think about sitting at a desk day in, day out…" He shook his head. "Being outdoors, that's my life."

"You never considered doing anything else?"

"Nope. I know every inch of this land. It's who I am."

"It sure is beautiful."

He pointed to the east. "See past that fence line? That's ten acres of prime land, some of the prettiest around here. It used to be a horse farm but it went belly-up last fall and the property went into foreclosure."

"I'm surprised no one was interested in buying it."

"Times are bad. I thought about purchasing

it and expanding the east pasture, but with this economy it's too much of a gamble. It would be perfect for a young couple, though. Build a house, raise a family. Maybe keep a horse or two."

Adam couldn't help wondering if he was talking about Katy. Was it possible she was she seeing someone? No, she would have told him. But realistically she wasn't going to stay single forever. She was going to find a good man. One willing to give her everything he couldn't. What she *deserved.*

"I understand you should be getting the DNA results soon," Gabe said, balling up the plastic from his sandwich and stuffing it in the paper sack from their lunch. "What do you plan to do if it's Katy's?"

The question put him on edge. Up until now they had avoided talking about Adam's relationship with Katy. But it was bound to come up. "I want to assure you that I'm going to take care of her and the baby. They won't ever want for anything."

"You know, it makes sense in a weird way. You fell in love with one of my daughters. I guess it's not so unusual you'd fall in love with the other one."

Love? Did he think…did he think Adam was going to *marry* Katy? "Katy and I…we don't have that kind of relationship."

"Is that why you two talk on the phone for hours practically every night?"

"Gabe—"

"And you can't keep your eyes off of her?"

"No disrespect to you or to Katy, sir, but I don't want to marry anyone."

"You've got something against marriage, son? I know Becca could be a handful, but—"

"Becca was a good wife. And the day I buried her, I swore it was something I would never do again."

Gabe took a swallow of his soda, then said, "So you'll spend your life alone instead? Sounds like a pretty miserable existence."

Not alone. He would have his child. "I don't see it that way."

Gabe shrugged, like it was no skin off his nose. "We should get busy. We have a lot to get done before supper."

He didn't want Gabe, or Katy's mom, deluding

themselves into thinking he was going to whisk Katy off her feet and carry her into the sunset. They would just have to get used to the idea of him and Katy being good friends.

Sixteen

Katy barely made it to three o'clock when she was so exhausted she had to lay down. And though she only planned on sleeping an hour or two, when she woke to the sound of the water running in the bathroom, it was almost six.

Her dad must have given Adam quite a workout if he needed a shower.

She knew she should get up, but she was so comfortable she didn't want to move. She curled in a ball, the tops of her thighs pressed against her belly. She was just starting to drift off when she felt it. A soft bump.

Her eyes flew open. Could that have been the baby kicking?

She lay there very still, waiting to see if it happened again. Then she felt it, a distinct kick. Maybe those flutters she'd been feeling had been the baby moving after all.

Nearly bursting with excitement, she rolled onto her back and pulled her shirt up so she could see her belly. It only took a few seconds before she felt another kick, and it was so hard this time she could actually see her stomach move!

She lay there frozen, afraid that if she moved the baby might stop, and she wanted Adam to feel it, too.

She heard the shower shut off and the sound of him tugging open the curtain.

"Adam! Get in here!" she called. "Hurry!"

Only a few seconds elapsed before the bathroom door swung open and Adam appeared, fastening a towel around his waist, hair mussed and still dripping. When he saw her lying there he must have thought the worst because all the color seemed to drain from his face. "What's wrong?"

"Nothing." She gestured him over. "Hurry, it's kicking."

He was across the room in a millisecond, and

perched on the edge of the mattress. "Are you sure?"

"Just watch," she said. "Right below my navel."

They waited several seconds then there was another quick bump-bump. "Did you see that?"

Adam laughed. "Oh, my God! Can I feel?"

She nodded, and he very gently placed his hand over her belly. His hand was warm from his shower and still damp. And there it was again, a soft little jab, as if the baby was saying, "Hey, I'm in here!"

She had been trying so hard to stay disconnected, to not think of it as *her* baby. But in that instant, feeling the baby move, she fell hopelessly in love. And she wanted it to be hers, so badly her heart hurt.

"What does it feel like to you?" he asked.

"Just like you would think. Like someone is poking me, but from the inside. I should call my mom in here so she can feel it."

"She's not here. She and your dad went out. She said they were going to catch a film in town and they would be back late."

They hardly ever went to the movies, so odds were good they were just giving Katy and Adam some time alone. They both seemed to have it in their minds that Adam was going to have a change of heart and suddenly decide that he loved her. What she didn't think they realized, what she hadn't realized until last night, was that he *did* love her. Even if he couldn't say it, she could see it in his eyes. And knowing that made his rejection a little easier to swallow for some reason. She wasn't damaged Katy, whom no one could love. Someone finally did. It just sucked that he was afraid to acknowledge it.

"It stopped," he said, sounding disappointed, but he didn't take his hand from her belly. And the fact that she was lying in bed wearing nothing but a shirt and panties, and he was only wearing a towel, started to sink in. Suddenly she felt hot all over and her heart was beating double time.

She would never know what possessed her, but she put a hand on his bare knee.

Dark and dangerous, his eyes shot to hers. "That's *not* a good idea."

Probably not. But for all the energy she'd spent convincing herself that this was never going to happen again, it didn't take much to have a total change of heart. And though she knew it was a mistake, and she was asking for heartbreak, she wanted him so much she didn't care what the repercussions would be.

She stroked his knee, scratching lightly with her nails.

"You're sending some pretty serious mixed signals," he told her, his voice uneven.

"Then let me be 100 percent clear." She slid her hand under the towel and up the inside of his thigh. He groaned and closed his eyes.

"I can't let you do this," he said, but he wasn't making an effort to stop her. And when her fingertips brushed against the family jewels he sucked in a breath and said in a gravelly voice, "Katy, stop."

"I can't. I want you, Adam. Even if it's just for a night or two."

He still wasn't ready to give in, so she took his hand that was still resting on her belly and guided it downward, between her thighs. "Touch me," she pleaded, and that was his undoing. He leaned over and kissed her. And kissed her and *kissed* her, and it was so perfect, she wanted to cry. He tugged the towel off and slid under the covers beside her. She expected it to be urgent and frenzied, like the night after she found out she was pregnant, but Adam took his time, kissing and touching her, exploring all the changes to her body, telling her she was beautiful. She'd never felt so sexy, so attractive, in her life. And when he made love to her it was slow and tender.

Afterward they lay curled in each others arms and talked. About work, and the baby, and the ranch—anything but their relationship.

Around ten she threw on her robe and went down to the kitchen to get them something to eat while Adam checked his phone messages. When she came back up with a plate of leftovers, Adam was dressed and shoving clothes into his duffel bag.

"You're leaving?" she asked.

"I'm sorry," he said. "I had a message from my COO. There's been an accident at the refinery."

"What kind of accident?"

"An explosion."

She sucked in a breath. "How bad?"

"Bad. At least a dozen men were hurt."

Katy's heart stalled. "How seriously?"

"Second- and third-degree burns."

"Oh, Adam, I'm so sorry."

"Since I took over, safety has been my number-one priority and we've had a near-spotless record. Not a single accident that required more than the need for a small bandage. Injured employees means negative press and lawsuits and OSHA investigations."

"So this could be bad?"

He nodded. "This could be very bad. But my main concern right now is making sure those men are being taken care of."

"What caused the explosion?" she asked.

"We're not sure yet." He sat on the bed to pull on his socks and boots. "They're still trying to put out the blaze. Jordan said they had just completed a maintenance cycle and were bringing everything back on line when something blew. Which makes no sense, because everything had just been thoroughly inspected." He rose from the bed and grabbed his duffel. "Katy, I am going to try like hell to be back in time for your appointment, but I just don't know if I can."

"Adam, don't even worry about that. If you can make it, fine, if not, there's always next month."

"Yes, but I've been saying that for two months now. I *want* to be there."

She smiled. "I know you do. That's why it's okay if you're not."

He dropped the duffel, gathered her up in his arms and planted a kiss on her that curled her toes and shorted out her brain. And if he didn't have to leave, man would he be in trouble.

"What was that for?" she asked when they came up for air.

"Because you're being so understanding."

"That's what you do when you love someone," she said.

It wasn't until she saw the stunned look on Adam's face, that she realized what she'd just said. How could she have just blurted it out like that?

And he obviously had no clue how to respond. It might have been amusing if she wasn't so mortified.

"Wow," she said, cheeks flaming with embarrassment. "I did not mean to just blurt that out."

"Katy—"

"Please," she said holding up a hand to stop him. "Anything you say at this point will only make it worse, and I'm humiliated enough. Just, please, let's pretend it never happened."

If there was any hope that he might have ever returned the sentiment, it died with his look of relief. "I really have to go."

"Go," she said, forcing a smile.

"We'll talk about this later." He gave her another quick kiss, then grabbed his duffel.

No, they wouldn't talk about it, she thought, as she listened to his heavy footfalls on the stairs, then the sound of the front door slamming. She resisted the urge to get up and watch him drive away. It would just be too hard, because it was a symbol. A symbol of the end of their relationship as she knew it. Not just their sexual relationship, but their friendship, as well.

Remaining friends after this would just be too...awkward. She didn't doubt that he knew she had strong feelings for him, maybe even loved him. But knowing it, and actually hearing the words were two very different things. He had no choice but to shut her out. She just hoped he would always be there for the baby.

And it occurred to her, as close as they had become these last few months, not only did she just lose her lover, but she'd also lost her best friend.

* * *

It never ceased to amaze Adam how, when his company did something positive, like adopting new and innovative environmentally friendly practices, he was lucky to get an inch on page twelve of the business section. But toss in a suspicious inferno, a few injured workers and an OSHA investigation and they'd made the front page of every national newspaper in the country. He personally had been hounded by the press at the office and even outside his home.

They had gone from being praised as having the most impressive safety record in the local industry to being labeled a deathtrap overnight.

Already they had been served with lawsuits by six of the thirteen injured men, the ones whose burns had been the most severe. The board, on the advice of their attorneys, had already agreed to settle the suits. It would set them back financially, but Adam was steadfast in his belief that it was the right thing to do. He was just thankful that no one was left permanently disabled, or, God forbid, killed.

Since the refinery had been in maintenance mode, the number of men on the line had been reduced by nearly half. The majority of the damage had been to the infrastructure. And now, every day they had to remain off line while the equipment was checked and rechecked, they lost hundreds of thousands of dollars in revenue.

Monday afternoon Adam called an emergency executive meeting in his office. OSHA had begun their investigation and it was beginning to look like the accident really wasn't an accident after all. If they ruled that it had been a case of gross negligence on the part of the men on the rig, the company would be slapped with a hefty fine.

Jordan, loyal to the death to his men, refused to believe they could possibly be responsible.

"My men work damned hard," he said, wearing a bare spot in the oriental rug with his pacing. Unusual considering he was by far the most laid-back of the four. "I would trust most of them with my life. There's no way they would be so careless. Not to mention that the entire line in question had just been thoroughly inspected. It doesn't make sense."

"Something about this does smell fishy to me," Nathan said. He sat in the chair opposite Adam's desk, looking troubled.

"You suspect foul play?" Adam asked.

"I say we shouldn't rule anything out. It would have to be an inside job, though."

Jordan stopped pacing to glare at his brother. "Impossible. Our people are loyal."

"Who then?" Nathan asked.

Jordan looked as though he wanted to deck him. "*Not* one of mine."

Adam didn't like the idea that one of his own employees could be responsible, but they had to know for sure, before there was another accident. "I think we need to hire our own investigator."

"We'll have to keep it quiet," Emilio, who had been standing by the window quietly observing, finally said. "If it was sabotage, and someone on the line is responsible, if they find out we're digging, any possible evidence will disappear. If he thinks he got away with it, he may be careless."

"Nathan," Adam said. "I want you in charge of this one."

"Why him?" Jordan scoffed, outraged. "I'm the one who understands the day-to-day operations. Those men trust me."

"Which is exactly why I'm assigning it to Nathan. It's going to get out eventually and you should have a certain degree of deniability. Not to mention that you're biased."

Jordan knew he was right. "Fine. But I want to be kept in the loop."

"Of course. If we do have suspects, you'll be in the position to keep a close eye on them, so this doesn't happen again. And I suppose it goes without saying that until this is resolved, I won't be stepping down as CEO. However long that takes. But that does *not* mean I won't be watching all of you."

"How is the pregnancy going?" Nathan asked.

"Great. In fact, I have to be back in Peckins tonight. Katy has her five-month checkup tomorrow." And he and Katy were long overdue for a serious discussion about the future of their relationship.

"Wait a minute," Jordan said. "You're actually leaving town? After everything that just happened?"

"I'll only be gone a day or two."

"What if we need you here?"

Jordan's reaction was understandable. Six months ago Adam wouldn't have dreamed of leaving town during a crisis. Not for a couple days. Not for five minutes. But his priorities had changed. Hell, his whole life had changed, and he had Katy and her family to blame. Or thank.

He kept thinking about what Gabe said, about how spending his life alone would be a miserable existence. Well, Adam *had* been miserable. For three years now. Until he got tangled up with Katy, he had genuinely forgotten what it felt like to be happy. To have something to look forward to.

Calling and asking her to meet him was one of the smartest things he'd ever done.

"We'll manage," Emilio said, sending Jordan a sharp look. "Can you two give me and Adam a minute?"

Nathan and Jordan left, and Emilio sat on the corner of Adam's desk.

"Okay, what's up?"

"What do you mean?"

"Jordan is right. You never leave during a crisis."

Emilio was going to find out eventually, so why not tell him now. "Something happened the other day when I was in Peckins. Something… unexpected. When I heard about the accident, I told Katy I had to leave, and said I might have to miss her appointment."

He winced. "You've missed two already."

"I know. And you know what she said?"

"I'm guessing it can't be good if it has you rushing back there."

"She said it was fine. That I could just go to the next one. She said knowing that I want to be there is good enough. And when I thanked her for being so understanding, she said that's what you do when you love someone."

Emilio's brow lifted. "She told you she loves you?"

He laughed. "Yeah, she just kind of blurted it out. And my first instinct, after I got over the surprise of her saying it, was that I love her, too."

"So did you tell her that?"

"I didn't get a chance. She got really embarrassed, and asked me to forget she said anything. I had to go. It didn't seem right to throw it out there, then leave."

"So you're going to tell her when you get there?"

"At this point, considering everything I've put her through, I don't think telling her is good enough, so I'm going to show her, too." Adam pulled the ring box out of his desk drawer and tossed it to Emilio.

Emilio laughed. "Is this what I think it is?"

Adam grinned.

He opened it and gave a low whistle. "I thought you were never getting married again, never taking the chance on burying another wife."

"It wasn't losing Becca that had made getting over her so hard. It was the regrets. The things we *didn't* say. And I can't go on pretending that we didn't have problems. Almost from the start."

"So why have kids?"

"I guess I thought that having a baby would fix everything. I thought it would bring us closer together. But honestly, it probably would have just made it worse. Neither one of us was very happy. If she hadn't gotten sick, I don't doubt we would be divorced by now."

He knew now that Celia was right, Becca *wasn't* his soul mate. She wasn't the love of his life, and he was pretty sure she sensed that.

"It's never easy admitting our mistakes," Emilio said.

"It's different with Katy. She's unlike anyone

I've ever known. She couldn't care less about my money. And if she thinks I'm acting like an ass, she isn't shy about saying so. She's everything I could possibly want or need in a wife. I can't even imagine my life without her in it."

"So what are you still doing here?" Emilio asked, tossing the ring back to Adam.

"It's only three."

"Yes, but you have a long drive ahead of you. Besides, we can handle things without you."

Emilio didn't have to tell him twice.

They weren't expecting company, so when Katy pulled up the driveway after a quick trip to the bank, she was surprised to see a car there. Before she got a good look she thought it might be Adam, but this was a dark sedan. A Mercedes, or BMW or something similar. And she knew Adam drove a red and sporty car.

She parked by the barn, thinking maybe they really did have a rich uncle. But she didn't have time to worry about that. She had a letter in her jeans pocket that could very well change the rest of her life. She got out and walked to the house, wondering who it could be. She went through the kitchen, the scent of home-fried chicken making her mouth water.

"Smells delicious, Elvie."

"That man is here," she whispered.

"What man?"

She nodded to Katy's belly. "The baby's father."

"*Adam* is here?" Elvie had to be mistaken.

She nodded, wide-eyed, and crossed herself. She was convinced, because Adam was so tall and dark and handsome, that he was *el Diablo* in the flesh.

She pushed through the kitchen door to the great room, expecting to see some man who looked like Adam sitting there with her parents, but it actually *was* Adam. And the instant she saw him, she knew all that stuff about them not being friends anymore was just bull.

When they heard her come in everyone turned in her direction.

She thrust her hands on her hips and asked Adam, "Exactly how many cars do you own?"

He grinned at her, then turned back to her parents and said, "I think that about covers it."

The three of them stood and her dad shook Adam's hand. Why would he do that?

"What's going on?" Katy asked them.

"Let's take a drive," Adam said.

"Why?"

"So we can talk."

"But it's almost suppertime."

"We won't be long."

Whatever he had to say must have been pretty bad if they had to leave the ranch. "Where are we going?"

"Not far." He crossed over to where she stood and took her hand, leading her to the front door. She looked back at her parents, but their expressions didn't give anything away.

Would he hold her hand—and in front of her parents—if he was about to tell her something awful? Or did he think it would soften the blow?

He opened the passenger door for her and she slid into the soft leather seat. He walked around and got in the driver's side, saying, as he started the engine, "Buckle up."

He waited until she was fastened in, then put the car into gear. It felt a little weird being in a car with him while he was actually behind the wheel. In the past it was always Reece driving.

Not that she expected him to be a terrible driver. It was just…different.

"How many cars do you own?" she asked as he made a left onto the road.

"Just the three."

They drove about a half a mile, then Adam made a sharp left and pulled up the road to the abandoned horse farm next door.

"What are we doing here?"

"I'll explain," he said cryptically.

The house and stables were in disrepair and the property overgrown, but it used to be a beautiful piece of land. And had the potential to be again someday. Her dad had talked about buying it, and she'd been disappointed when he changed his mind. Though she had never admitted it to anyone, she had even considered purchasing it. She had enough for a down payment in the bank. She just didn't like the idea of living alone.

Adam parked in a clearing by the stable and they got out. The sun was just beginning to set and there was a chill in the air.

"Are you warm enough?" he asked.

She nodded. He took her hand again and they walked slowly toward the stables. "Does this mean you're staying for my appointment tomorrow?"

The question seemed to surprise him. "Of course. Why would I drive all this way and not go?"

She shrugged.

"What do you think of this land?" he asked her.

"It's nice. Perfect for a small horse farm."

"What would you think if I said I bought it?"

She stopped in her tracks. "What? Why?"

He grinned. "So I could build a house here. And probably a new stable."

"You're serious?"

"Yep."

Well, if the baby was hers, and he was going to be visiting a lot, didn't it make sense that he had somewhere to stay? But they weren't even sure yet.

They started walking again, past the stables and along the corral fence, the overgrown grass and weeds grabbing at her pant legs. "I think that sounds like a good investment."

"So you wouldn't mind living here?"

Living here? He was going to build a house for *her?* Did he know something she didn't? Had the lab sent him a letter, too, and had he read it? After they agreed they would look at the results *together.*

"Adam, what's going on?"

They stopped where the corral turned, near an apple tree that had probably been there longer than the house. "This should do," Adam said.

"Do for what?"

"There are a few things I have to tell you, Katy."

She swallowed hard, bracing for the worst, her hands clammy she was so nervous.

"We had to launch an investigation into the accident at the refinery, and as soon as it's resolved, I'm leaving Western Oil."

For a full ten seconds she was too dumbfounded to speak. And when she found her voice, it was uncharacteristically high-pitched. "Leaving? As in quitting?"

"I'll still be on the board, but I'm stepping down as CEO."

"W-why?"

"It's time. I want to be around to see my child grow up."

"That's wonderful," she said, wondering what that meant for her, if it meant anything at all.

"Remember the other night, when you said you love me?"

She cringed, still mortified that she had actually done something so stupid. "I thought we agreed not to talk about that."

"You issued an order, and I didn't agree to anything."

It was obvious he wasn't willing to let it go. He was going to torture her. "Okay, what about it?"

"I'll admit I was a little stunned—"

"You were way more than stunned. And I don't blame you, Adam. It was wrong of me to put you on the spot like that."

He took a deep breath and exhaled. "Can I finish?"

She nodded, even though she knew she wasn't going to like what he had to say.

"I was in a hurry to leave, but if I'd had more than thirty seconds to think about it, I would have told you that I love you, too."

He heart climbed up into her throat. She had never expected him to admit it, to say it out loud.

"Aren't you going to say anything?" he asked.

"I...I don't know what to say."

"You could say that you love me, too."

Unable to look in his eyes, and see the sincerity there, she looked down at the ground instead. "You already know that."

"I *need* you, Katy."

For now. But what about a month from now? He didn't want to get married, and she couldn't accept any less than that.

She wanted forever.

Adam bent down on one knee in the weeds. She thought he was going to pick something up off the ground, then she saw that he already had something in his hand.

"What are you doing?"

"Something I should have done months ago." He opened his hand and sitting on his palm was a black velvet box. It actually took her several seconds to figure out what was happening. Then she started to tremble so hard she wasn't even sure her legs would hold her up.

Adam opened the box to reveal a stunning diamond solitaire ring. He looked up at her and grinned, "Marry me, Katy?"

"You're serious?"

"I've never been more sure of anything in my life."

"But...Becca—"

"Is gone. Becca was my wife, and I loved her, but I didn't need her the way I need you. You're my soul mate. I don't want to go another day, another minute, knowing you aren't going to be mine forever."

She'd imagined this moment so many times in her head, but none of her fantasies compared to the real thing, and she'd be damned if she was going to give him even a second to change his mind.

She threw herself in his arms so hard that they lost their balance and tumbled backward in the weeds.

He laughed and said, "Should I take that as a yes?"

"Definitely yes," she said, kissing him, wondering if this was a dream. Was it even possible to be *this* happy?

Adam sat them up and pulled her into his lap. "Would you like this now?" he asked, holding up the ring box.

She'd almost forgotten! "Will you put it on me?"

He took it from the box and slid it on her finger. It was a perfect fit. "I have *huge* fingers. How did you guess the size?"

"I didn't. I asked your mom."

"When?"

"Sunday morning."

Katy's mouth fell open. "She's known about this since *Sunday?*"

"I didn't tell her why I needed it, but I think she had a pretty good idea."

Suddenly it made sense why he was sitting there with her parents when she walked in, and why her dad shook his hand. "Oh, my gosh, did you ask my parents' *permission?*"

"I thought it would be a nice touch, since I kind of missed that step last time. I figured they deserved it."

She threw her arms around his neck and hugged him, the baby pressed between them. That's when she remembered the letter in her pocket. They were together now, and no matter whose baby it was, she would be raising it. But he deserved to know the truth.

"I have to show you something," she said, pulling the letter out. "This came in today's mail."

"The DNA results?"

She nodded.

He took the letter from her, and for a minute he just looked at it, then he looked up at her, shrugged and said, "I don't care."

"You don't care?"

He took her hands. "What difference do genetics make? This is *our* baby, Katy. Yours and mine. Either way, it's a miracle. So unless you really need to know—"

"I don't," she said. "Though I tried to be impartial, and not get attached, I've felt like this baby has been mine pretty much from the day it was conceived."

With a smile on his face, Adam ripped the envelope in two, then into fourths, then he kept on ripping until there was nothing left but scraps, then he tossed them in the air.

Katie couldn't help wondering, though...would she ever be curious? Someday would she want to know?

But the following spring, when Amanda Rebecca Blair was born—a healthy eight pounds seven ounces—and Katy held her daughter for the first time, she knew without a doubt that it would never matter.

* * * * *

 *Mills & Boon® Online*

Discover more romance at
www.millsandboon.co.uk

- **FREE** online reads
- **Books** up to one month before shops
- **Browse our books** before you buy

...and much more!

For exclusive competitions and instant updates:

 Like us on **facebook.com/romancehq**

 Follow us on **twitter.com/millsandboonuk**

 Join us on **community.millsandboon.co.uk**

Visit us Online   Sign up for our FREE eNewsletter at
www.millsandboon.co.uk

WEB/M&B/RTL4/LP